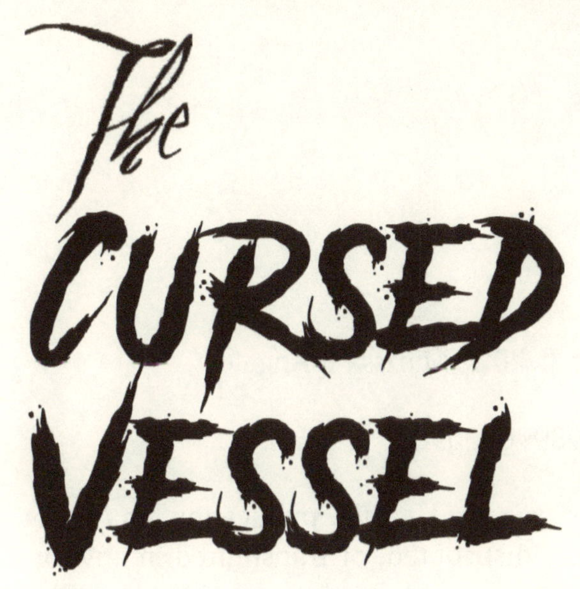

The CURSED VESSEL

A TALE OF CHARLES ISLAND

MARISSA D'ANGELO

Dedication

This book is dedicated to my dad who taught me that no matter what, everyone deserves a chance. Everyone deserves to be given the benefit of the doubt. This book is for all the troublemakers who are trying to find their place in the world; you belong.

Let fate bring you where you are meant to be.

Books by Marissa D'Angelo

Tales of Charles Island Series

The Cursed Spirit

The Cursed Spirit 2

The Cursed Vessel

The Cursed Inn

The Cursed Monastery

Presence

Other Books

The Vanished

Chasing Time

Author's Note

Since the release of this book, I have wanted to find some way to help Charles Island and the wildlife that it supports. A local reforestation group is working hand in hand with the Connecticut Department of Energy and Environmental Protection to plant more trees so that the island and its wildlife can survive and thrive.

Message from Reforestation Group:

We want to restore the island to its former state. After years of invasive species and diseases, we need to help nature along with this task.

<u>10% of the proceeds from this series will go to this cause.</u>

The Dream

1

Steady seas made for the perfect day of sailing. Persistent swishing of the waves as they gently came in against the sandy shores, they carried multiple shells back to sea with them again and again. When the sun peeked out of the puffy white clouds, it urged me all the more to be out there. I longed to be with the shipmates, even starting out as I did one of the worst crew-mate jobs of scrubbing the deck floors or cooking for hours on end. I could hear the floorboards creak as

I walked down the deck, introducing myself to the captain who would likely care less. Seagulls swarming the skies, letting out a screech for their own friend had taken their catch of the day. This reminded me much of humans for many would take credit for the other's work or steal their earnings and keep them as their own. This was all a dream of mine though. I would find myself up on this hill, peering out at the ships - thinking of how different my life would be if I had the life of a crewmate. But that was just the first step. My desire to someday be captain was the true endpoint that I aimed for most. There was something about letting the wind guide your sail to and fro. A natural sense of curiosity came just from the very idea of one day having a ship of my own. A crew of my own. To voyage anywhere I wanted at any given time and have that freedom.

Each and every day, I would wake up and sneak out of my house to run up the hill to watch the sunrise. Smooth blurs of orange crept over the horizons, illuminating it in an ethereal glow as if the very edge of earth was on fire. Instead, everything in the glow's path radiated in warmth and light. In the small town of Greenock, a picturesque landscape of mountains and valleys made up the surrounding territories aside from the lone village. Port Glasgow thrived with imports and exports - colossal ships came and went each and every day. It seemed that everyone was in a constant state of bustling around every which way. Even from the roads, you could see the ships' masts poking over roofs of houses along the way. As I climbed up the small hill near my home to watch that sunrise, I remember watching the ships in awe and utter admiration for its crew. As soon as the sun came into full view from the horizons, I jumbled back down the hill to get home before it was noticed that I snuck out. Peering down the roads, I could see father in the top floor's window, extending both his arms up and out for a nice morning stretch. At that point, I stopped - backing up against the cold, brick wall that belonged to a building adjacent, as to not be caught out.

Peering around the corner of where I had just stood, I saw that father was no longer in the window and I ran towards the back of the house as fast as I could. That gave me just a few moments before he would be downstairs and looking for me. Beside our house, our neighbors always kept various types of flowers. Tall stalks of thistle shot out from the ground and leaned towards the sun that had just made its appearance in the sky. Contrasting to the towering stalks were delicate bluebells, which were also purple despite their name, but delicately poked out of the dew-covered grasses. Mother resembled the bluebells most. She would wake every morning before father and scurry downstairs to set a proper table with the meager portions of food that we were able to afford as a family. I did not resemble her in the slightest if not for the light green eyes that she passed down to me. I grabbed a bunch of bluebells and headed up the back steps. Mother was in on my secret as long as I didn't get caught from father. I tried my best to sneak inside through the back door, but the creaking steps announced my presence. Before I could grasp the handle of the door in my fingers, it swung open and father stood in the doorway, eyebrows furrowed down.

"Boy, you must not venture out there without us knowing. We've told you that time and time again," I looked over at mother and saw her sympathetic face as she too must have had a dream similar to mine. But the difference with me, was that I was not going to let anything come in the way of that dream. Father must have noticed my gaze as I looked over at her instead of him and he too looked back at mother who broke her eye contact from me and continued cleaning after breakfast.

"Don't think she's going to help you, if you're going to be the man of this family you've got to straighten up," he said, rigidly.

The man of the family. What a joke. That didn't seem to work very well for him. He followed everything that he was supposed to do and listened to his superiors except we still were left with scraps of food each night

despite all of his struggles each day. I would be the man

of the family, but I would actually come through.

School Days

2

The bells sounded, signifying an alarm that it was time to come to school. Its chime sounded throughout the entirety of the village, bellowing down each road and alleyway. You could hear it above the blaring horns of ships arriving to deliver various exports and goods. What I would do to be there. Nonetheless, I found myself hurrying along the outskirts of town, heading towards the bells. I was no different than a cat running towards its home when the dinner bells rang -

collecting scraps and remnants of food from the humans that allowed them to reside there. Most would see them as a nuisance, but they kept the rats and other vermin away. Because of this, I grew incredibly fond of them and would allow them to follow me home as they expected any leftovers to be given to them from what I had for that night's supper. Now, they likely slept as they seemed to be nocturnal creatures - lurking the streets at night, hunting after their prey. I thought if I ever became a ship captain, I would surely have one of those cats. At least one... or maybe two so that the one could keep the other company.

"Hey there, William! Wait up!" A familiar voice rang out from one of the side alleyways. I continued pacing towards the schoolhouse but turned back slightly to find Patch chasing after me. His wispy blonde hair blew back as he followed, trying to catch up. Freckles swarmed the entirety of his light skin and as his face spread into a mischievous smile, dimples appeared on both cheeks. Like me, he wore ragged shorts and a plain shirt that was a hand-me down from other children that were now grown and didn't fit into the unwanted clothes any longer. They would likely be passed down until they were no longer distinguishable as clothes and instead looked like rags which is what they were just beginning to resemble.

My pace turned into a jog and as Patch realized what I was doing and also mirrored my movements, I sprinted towards the obnoxious bells. It turned into a game as he raced after trying to catch me, but we did this very often and he could never... ever catch me no matter how hard he tried. Mothers, that had just sent their children off to school, shook their heads as we passed by them, nearly knocking their younger children over completely.

"You'll never catch me!" I yelled back through heavy breaths as I continued towards the school. In a flurry of uncontrollable laughter, I felt tears streaming from the corners of my eyes and my vision suddenly blurred. Before I knew it, I was stopped dead in my tracks from Mrs. Sarabella. She held out her long arm, which I ran into, thus knocking me back onto the ground. I looked up her way and blinked a few times, innocently. It was nothing but a game, after all. Just a little fun. I looked back at Patch and he was no longer running either as he started walking past us to go into the schoolhouse.

"Don't think about it," Mrs. Sarabella's stern tone halted him in his tracks as well.

"Don't you all realize what you've done??!" We looked at each other and simultaneously shook our heads upon turning our attention back towards our teacher. She just didn't understand fun, but I don't think that's what she was focusing on now…when I followed her gaze, I saw several children disheveled and fallen over that we must have stormed past in our race against one another.

"Well?" She asked, expecting some sort of response or reason why I had done what I did. But that's the thing, I had no reason. Instead of supplying her with a sufficient explanation as to why I did what I did, I shrugged my shoulders. We were given a brief lecture about the rules which I could've probably recited in my sleep and all I could hear in my head while she spoke was "Blah, blah, blah, blah…" After her never ending speech, we followed Mrs. Sarabella into the schoolhouse.

- - - - - - - -

After teaching us about Christianity and reading parts of the bible to us, I was just becoming comfortable where I sat. Gradually, my eyelids grew heavier and heavier. So heavy that I could no longer keep them open. At one moment, the teacher was pointing to her chalkboard at a line that she had previously written down and in the next, the chalky letters turned into swirls and spirals of open ways on a map that I now analyzed to embark on my next voyage. The farthest point of which outlined the map was my endpoint. I would follow the darkest of paths with my crew and lead them to land that hadn't been previously explored.

New land that our feet would be the first to meet and

discover. What kinds of animals would they have?

Would there be trees full of fruits? In the grasses, would

I see bluebells that reminded me of my mother and the

tall, poky thistle that resembled father? Patch would be

my mate on this journey along with some cats that we

would keep on our ship to get rid of vermin. After

looking through the map, I traced one of the routes,

drawing an arrow towards my endpoint. An island

would surely be there! When Patch and I had gathered

enough of a crew, we all agreed upon our destination

and they were the most loyal crew that I ever had. Using

a gold compass that I was given from my grandfather,

we drew away from the docks and the steady rocking of

our ship sent me into a lull while others became seasick.

They would eventually grow used to it the more often we traveled. When we first embarked, the cool breeze hit the opaque sail and I hollered to Patch to undo more sails so that we could let the wind guide us further. And further. Until the land around us faded. What once were colossal mountains now appeared to be much smaller and hill-like until they were no longer visible at all.. Eventually, the horizons disappeared and everything around us was just open sea. Where this would frighten some, it thrilled me in every way. I just wanted more. I couldn't get enough. The once steady and calm waves picked up as the sky darkened and enveloped us in a grey, monotonous aura. Waves rocked the deck back and forth; some eventually grew big enough to send water up and onto the main floorboards.

"Captain, we've hit a storm!" Some of my crew mates yelled as they began taking over the sails. Heavy rain dropped down all at once and felt like harsh bullets as they ripped through my ship. It seemed that the entire vessel was shaking and before I could reach out to grab onto the side so that I could support my balance, there was a long wooden object that came out of nowhere and started tapping. It wouldn't stop. The tapping grew louder until I couldn't take it any longer.

"What? Where am I?" I called out, opening my eyes to find Mrs. Sarabella standing closer to me than she had before, this time holding a long stick. That must've been what the wooden object was. The rest of the class laughed at my response, but her expression remained unchanged. She shot a glare back at the other kids and they quickly stopped their laughter. She pointed to the door and when I stayed seated where I had just entered a nice slumber, she pointed a second time. With her persistence, I finally gave in and stood up... heading out of the schoolhouse. That was my very last day of school you could say. Little did I know that was going to be the last day of my childhood despite being thirteen years of age.

Growing Up

3

"You can't work here, you're just a kid! Go back to school," my third attempt at a job down the drain... I had accepted to do the dishes for anyone just for a few coin. If I thought things were hard previously, I was out of my mind. It had been several months since that day when the teacher sent me out of school and I found out the news. I came home after being thrown out of school for my mischief and laziness only to find my mother on her hands and knees just before the front entrance of our home. She was sobbing uncontrollably as locks of her dirty blonde hair pressed to her skin, wet from her tears. As she knelt against the creaky step in the back that I would commonly use to sneak in the house, she looked even more frail than I had ever seen her before. Resembling the width of a toothpick, she barely grasped the rails that stood over the steps. It looked as though she was about to go inside when she found out whatever news that crippled her. I couldn't run to her side fast enough and wrapped my arms around her as she shook. I had never seen her like this before and was afraid to ask what happened. There was no simple answer as to what to do. I just wanted to see her smile again like when she would while shaking her head at something I did wrong. *Did I do something wrong again? Was this because of me?* Maybe the teacher got the news to her that I had been kicked out of school.

I pulled away from her, realizing the damage that I had done.

"Mother, I'm sorry about what I did," I admitted, regretfully. She didn't look up and continued sobbing. "I was just so tired," I added. There was really no excuse, but here I was holding onto any ounce of explanation that I could find for her. Sharp inhales and gasps filled the air in an urgent, distressed tone.

"It's nothing that you did," she said. "Your father passed away at his job this morning. It was sudden. There was no pain for him." Before I was able to realize it, I felt my legs collapse beneath me and found myself on the ground… in the dirt where I belonged. I couldn't breathe; there was a giant pit in my stomach that reminded me of the emptiness that now overcame me.

An emptiness that nothing would be able to fill. My palms felt sweaty and cold at the same time. Legs numb and bent beneath where I lay. I could hear sobbing from mother again as she clearly didn't know what else to do. There was nothing to do or say. Confusion cut deep and my mind started wandering to all sorts of thoughts. Father was only ever trying to make things easier for me and for us, but I was up to some type of mischief, always. I began to dig in the dirt and sand with my bare hands. A hole in the ground was where I belonged. I continued digging as fast as I could. Dirt pushed under my nails and my hands where no longer a rosy, white. They had turned pale, but now they were brown with dirt. Above, the sky opened up and let crashing drops of rain come down all at once. There was no warning of this just as there hadn't been with father. My father.

As the wet drops moistened the dirt beneath me, it made it all the easier to continue digging a hole. The continuous sobbing from mother had ceased and now the only sound that remained was that of the rain hammering down on our village.

- - - - - - - - -

So there I was, trying my best to fulfill the position that my father left open. Mother tried to get work, too, but it was no use because the majority of our coin came from him even if it was very little. I had tried at all of the local fisheries and other places for a job but had no luck anywhere because I "should be at school." When I told mother that I was going to get a job instead of going back to school, she nodded her head in agreement. We both knew that I was better working with my hands anyway even for a thirteen-year-old.

My last resort at a job was to check with the boaters and crews in case they had the need for a cleaner or any type of position at all. Instead of going up the hill this time, I made my way through my village and down the hill that several houses rested upon. Rocky paths that had been ridden over by horse and carriage led me down to the port of our town. A towering hand-carved piece of wood stood raised by a pole at the very entrance to this port. From my frequent visits to the hilltop, the pole appeared to be much smaller, but at this point I saw how impressive it truly was. A literate person…maybe Mrs. Sarabella, likely etched in letters on the sign. Gold trails of words spelled out: PORT GLASGOW. A horse and carriage came rushing by without hesitation or pause to see if I was crossing the street. I was nearly thrown back and as they went, the chains that held the sign on, blew back and forth causing a jingle. In the middle stretch of the port were grown men with ragged clothes on. They looked soaking wet as if they had just gone for a dip in the water, but it must have been from their sweat. All too fast, men held boxes on each shoulder and others rolled barrels of what was likely wine. I remembered seeing father at one of the village parties as he took a cup and filled it with the deep maroon drink. None of the men resembled father. Even though they were tall, their clothes were covered in stains; they had long beards and hair as well. Father kept his hair short and would always shave his face, never revealing a beard.

Am I really going to go up to one of these men and ask to work for them? The men that had been rolling barrels went past me and loaded them into a wagon. They were completely unaware of my presence. I began to back away when I saw the light purple flowers poking out of the grass. Their delicate nature reminded me. There are things that we have to do for those that we love even if they are difficult. And even those things aren't entirely done for the people whom we love because they are partly done for ourselves. When we take care of our loved ones, we take care of ourselves too because we feel good seeing them happy and safe. Bluebells. Mother. Without any hesitation this time, I continued down towards the docks. I could hear the men following closely behind as they likely wondered what I was doing there. They came so close that they ended up walking around me. As they passed, I could feel the sweat beading off their skin and the heat radiated from their close proximity. All looked strikingly similar, however there was one that trailed behind and had light brown hair as opposed to the dark that the others had. He trailed behind them and walked beside me as I made my way over to one of the boats. I attempted not to make eye contact, but it was too difficult with how close he stood to me.

"Well, hello," I said. I wasn't scared of him. His response was a grin as he didn't seem to expect me to say anything.

"I know exactly who you are, William Kidd, huh?" He stopped in his tracks and put a hand on each hip. And who was he?

"Who told you that?" I urgently wanted to know more. There was no reason that he should know my name and of all people, I was a no one. Ok, let me change that. I was a troublemaker in town… a bit of a troublemaker, but I meant good and I always paid my debts.

"I meet Mrs. Sarabella from time to time and oh has she had a lot to say about you!" He started to chuckle as if he said the funniest thing all day. Well, there goes my chance. She has ruined my name in this entire town, hasn't she…?

"I decided that line of work is not cut out for me and instead I'm trying my hand at being a crew-mate of some sort," I spoke in all honesty. This only made him chuckle all the more. All of the laughing was getting to be awfully annoying to me and I started walking again.

If he wasn't going to take me seriously, then I would find someone who would.

"Wait up!!" He called after me and eventually caught up. "We do have some men that left the cleaning crew to stay on land with their maidens. Maybe you could start there?" He suggested. I nodded my head and followed him. Maybe talking to this man wasn't so useless after all.

Goodbye

4

After talking for a while, I found out that the man who I was following joined life at sea when he was just a young lad, too. In his case, he had no choice because his entire family had died of disease and he was the only to remain. Outcasted by his village due to the death of his family, they all thought of him to be of bad luck. His name was Jack after his father and grandfather. It was quite possible that every man in the family bore that name and as a sign of respect, they kept it. In my mind, it was out of laziness - they don't have to think of a new name for a child if one is already chosen and they can continue reusing it. There was an aspect to this that made sense, though. Naming your kin after you showed how one would live on through their children. It made me feel better that I wasn't the first boy to do this who hadn't reached adulthood. If it was done before then that meant it was possible. And possible I could do.

We approached one of the ships and he threw a rope over to me that he had been holding. The interwoven ends felt almost as harsh as sandpaper against my palms. I turned each part around again and again, wrapping it in a circle so that it was easier to hold and not trip over. Jack reached up to the closest ledge of the ship and extended his hand out to me.

"Here, take my hand," he said. In the back of my mind I felt as though I could easily be taken prisoner. I wouldn't make much of a prisoner... if they had a ransom, there would be no one to pay it. I decided I wouldn't be taken prisoner since it wouldn't be worth it to either party. Taking his hand was difficult as I felt the sweat seep into my own skin and squeezed tight so that I wouldn't slip out of his grasp. He somehow managed to pull me aboard the ship.

Darkened floorboards set out all around me. The creaks after each step reminded me of the wooden stairs by the back door of my home. Memories of the many sunrises and sunsets that I'd sneak out to watch swarmed through my mind. At sea, I'd always be able to watch this no matter what and it showed me that no matter where I was, I wasn't truly that far away from my loved ones for they too could watch. We could be thousands of miles away from one another, yet so close at the same time. The crew had barely noticed that I jumped aboard their ship at first. They were still occupied with their imports as they passed crates and barrels down to others on land so that they could haul them out. I knew that Jack wasn't the captain, but I needed his approval in order to set out to sea with him so I followed Jack towards the captain's cabin like a duckling waddling after its mother.

"Everyone, this is...William! William Kidd! He can help us out with our deck since we lost the others," Jack called out as we headed there.

No one stopped what they were doing to even acknowledge me as if many would often come and go from the crew so they were used to it. No use getting to know just another person who they'd have to part with at any time. When we went past the main mast, I felt overwhelmed and exhilarated all at once. Even in my dreams, I had never imagined it to appear so strong and colossal in size. The sail had been taken down since they were docked, but I could hardly wait to see it put back up, taking the wind in as we glided out to sea.

A knock snapped me out of my daze and Jack persistently pounded his knuckles against the door of what presented to be the captain's cabin. I continuously rubbed my palms against the sides of my pants, anxious at what he would say about me joining the crew. This was the last attempt that I had before it meant we lost our home because we could no longer afford its expense.

"Yes, yes!!" A round man came jumbling out of the door, wobbling all over the place. His dark red shirt hung down too far to meet his waistline as it went just past his knees similar to a dress. He wore long pants underneath the red shirt that came down considerably low for a man of his stature. To my surprise, he was almost as short as me which meant that I would surely tower over him in a few years. This was not what I expected when I thought of the word, "captain."

"Harry, this is William. William Kidd. He's looking for work, I thought I'd run it by Cap't first," he was cut short. As soon as the wobbling man walked away, the captain walked out from behind him. Unlike the rest of his crew that were barely distinguishable, he had a clean-shaven face. His rosy-white skin reminded me of my own, but he had freckles all over his face. The multitude of freckles were strikingly similar to my school friend, Patch. Dirty blonde hair went down almost to his chest, reminding me of Mrs. Sarabella.

"Captain!!!" The round man screamed, not realizing that he was right next to him. I could smell the wine from his strained breaths. The gent who was referred to as "captain," patted his friend on the shoulder as if he was used to this behavior. He looked me up and down and I stood as tall as I could, partially lifting the heels of my feet up so that I could appear even more elevated. It looked as though captain was fighting to smile, the corner of his mouth drawn up in a smirk.

"Well…we need the help. But I swear, the one time that I am having to parent you, you're off the ship. You hold your own out here and don't get into any trouble," he said. I gulped. It was quite often that trouble found a way into my life, but there had to be some way to manage life without it.

"Yes, you've got it." I agreed, holding out my hand. He took it in his and we had a deal.

"We leave at sunset and if you're not here, don't count on us to wait for you," he said and wasting no time, walked back into his quarters.

"See, what did I tell you?!" Jack reassured me even though I felt like it was going to be difficult to earn the captain's trust. We started walking along the main deck and instead of most of the crewmen ignoring my presence, they looked over at me and then one another. There must have been an inside joke between them because as soon as they met one another's gaze, they all started cracking up.

"Hey, what's so funny?!" Jack glared over at them.

"Oh, we are just so grateful to have a child boarding our ship. He'll surely be a great crewmate," one of them said sarcastically. Jack scoffed and we continued walking.

"Don't mind them, they'll warm up to you eventually. We're all family here," he said and patted me on the back a few times.

"I guess we ran into each other at the right time. There's just one thing that I have to do before I come back here. I'll see you in a little while," I shook Jack's hand and realized that my palms were no longer sweaty. It was as if a weight had been lifted off my shoulders through the acceptance of setting sail with the others. As I headed off the main deck, I used the rope ladder that hung down the side to get back to land. The pit in my chest that had formed when I lost father was already starting to come back. It had been filled the moment I stepped on the ship and that's how I knew that the path I was taking was meant to be. After casually walking back up the hill towards my village, I picked up my pace faster and faster. Feeling my feet run like wild, I couldn't wait to tell mother the news. It was bittersweet, but I knew that she would understand. After all, she shared my dream of being out to sea and would likely push her feelings aside so that I could live my dream. In what felt like nearly thirty minutes, I made it to the back door and crept up the steps. When I walked in, she was sitting at the table with her face in her hands. She looked miserable and like she had been crying. As soon as she heard the wooden steps creak on my way in, she jumped up and headed over to the sink to do dishes. It was almost as if she put on a mask for she didn't want me to see her in that state. At once, I hesitated to tell her, but then thought it would perhaps cheer her up.

"Mother, I have news! I have news!" I blurted out, unable to wait another moment. I reached into the pail of water that she washed the dishes in and wrapped my hands around hers. Her eyes were bright with curiosity and likely mirrored my own as it looked like she had been waiting for some excitement all day.

"The captain down at one of the ships in Port Glasgow hired me as one of the crewmen. One of them, Jack, showed me around and referred me over to him!" I said without sparing a minute to breathe. What once was a shining gleam of light coming from her eyes turned down into a sullen, dull look full of sadness.

"Hey, I am going to come back! This just means that I will get payment and can bring it back to you. Mom, I am one less mouth to feed, too!" I said, trying to be realistic.

I shuddered as this reminded me too much of my father. Gone were the days when I had time to think from my heart and now I had to face that this was a part of my destiny that had to play out.

"You promise?" She said, looking up at me again with a half-smile. As hard as it was for us, we both knew that I had to do this. The village people were close to one another and our neighbors who planted the thistle and bluebells always invited mother over so that she wouldn't have to be alone. This didn't make leaving much easier, but it helped to give some comfort of knowing that she would be okay and looked after. I gave her a long hug and she helped me pack my things for the first journey I would ever take off land and the beginning of a new life that I had always dreamed of.

"One last thing," she mentioned before I set off to board the ship. Behind her back, she pulled out a book that I hadn't recognized right away. As I walked over, she opened it midway to reveal some fresh-picked bluebells. I took the open book in my hands and looked up at her, a tear streaming down my cheek. I had told myself that I wouldn't cry as I was sure it would cause the same tears from her eyes. She wiped her cheek with a napkin.

"I want you to have this Bible and remember me. When you feel that you are alone, just know that you are not. In your heart, you have both your father and I," she got down on her knees as I stood there not knowing what to say. The book trembled in my hands as I felt the world could open up and swallow me whole at any second. Without warning, she closed the book in my hands and pulled out a gold compass that father said I could have long ago once I was old enough.

"May this guide you back to wherever home is whenever you find you have lost your way in life," she put it in my pocket and stood back up to kiss my forehead. A sincere kiss that sent an everlasting warmth through my body and made me want to never leave home again. But then I remembered who I was and just the mere fact that I would embark on this journey was the first step in making my dream come true.

Newfound Family

5

Many years had passed and the crew that I set sail with ended up becoming a long-lost family to me. The empty pit that ran deep within my core remained but was buried by the many responsibilities that now piled upon me on a daily basis. Busy meant keeping out of trouble. At first, I had just been assigned to scrubbing the floors and fetching things for Captain Oliver. As the years passed, I eventually became his righthand man beside his crewmate, Harry. For some reason, his trust in me grew in just a short time even though he had been cold in the very beginning. We would stop back at Port Glasgow to carry imports in as well as load the ship with various exports. When we'd stop there, I would have a chance to visit mother. Each time, she looked more and more frail. I would save up all the coin I had to give to her so that she was able to pay for our home. She hadn't thought that I would come back and my first visit was such a shock that she nearly fell over where she sat. To my surprise, she pulled off the ring from her finger and handed it to me. Father gave this to her and was the finest piece of jewelry she owned. It very well may have been the only piece of jewelry she had.

"I forgot to give this to you and worried you wouldn't come back so that I could leave it with you!" She exclaimed.

"Mother, there are no women out at sea..." I said, blushing at the fact that she thought I was ready to take someone's hand in marriage.

"Nonsense! You never know," if it weren't for her dazzled eyes gleaming up at me, I would've continued questioning her. However, she looked so hopeful that I couldn't deny her the happiness of leaving the ring with me. Each time that we came back to Port Glasgow, she would ask if I gave the ring away yet and I hadn't. When I headed back onto the ship to set sail for another voyage, I took on the job as an apprentice cook. Having never cooked before, I learned from Jack who was actually quite good at baiting fish in from the seas and frying them up. This earned me two times the salary that I had previously made. Captain Oliver believed in me and saw past what my teachers had previously pointed out as failures.

Some nights, I would listen in on all of the stories that the crew had to share. Most of them would drink as much as they could while I cleaned up after them. When the dark skies were clear and calm seas surrounded us, we would light a fire in a small, empty barrel. The crew would take a break from what they were doing and sit around it. Even Captain Oliver would join in on the conversation. I remember I usually stayed away from their get together, but as I grew older - they included me more and more. It all started when Jack overheard me as one step on the wooden deck caused the creaky floorboard to sound, alerting them that I was there. He signaled his hand over as if to ask me to join them. From then on, I was always invited to their stories. After pouring some drinks for them all, I would sit beside Jack.

There was one story that I will never forget that captured my curiosity to the point that I would dream often about it. Captain Oliver was the one to tell this tale. He walked over from his cabin and filled his cup up as high as it would go without overflowing. As he pushed both of his cuffs up so that his forearms were exposed, it was clear that he was going to tell us something serious. We all leaned in to listen to what he had to say. The fire between us illuminated his face as well as everyone else's. But because he was the closest as he paced around, his shone the most.

"Want to hear the story of the forbidden island?" He asked. Most of the men were drinking and continued doing so while nodding their heads. I was one of the few to verbally call out.

"Yes," I exclaimed.

Stories of the sea were some of my favorites and those were the ones that I would not fall asleep during. Captain Oliver looked over at me and smiled, expecting this response from me.

"We had traveled to the new land of America. Several settlers had been venturing out there to create a new civilization..." he paused and took a swig from his cup.

"There were people there before the Europeans... long before the Europeans these natives called America home. If anything, we are all intruders to them… these people do not speak our tongue," he continued.

"Have you met them?" I asked, unable to control my thoughts. He nodded in response.

"Briefly. It is best for us to stay away from one another, but they did try to help by supplying us with something they hold sacred: corns, beans and squash. There was an island that was fully forested with an abundance of trees. A pathway that washed up perfectly at low tide revealed a direct route there. The whistling winds called out to me and I felt that I was destined to walk to this mysterious place. During the day, I figured it was harmless and even brought some of my knives anyway just in case. I made it about halfway there when one of the natives, a girl around twenty-five or so years of age ran out to me urgently yelling. She must have picked up some of the tongue from the Europeans as she shouted, 'No, No, No!'" He walked over to the edge of the ship to look out for a moment. He appeared to be reminiscing on the past memory that seemed to be long ago.

"I stopped in my tracks and it was hard to take her seriously because after all, it was just an island. The first thought that came into my mind was that maybe the land belonged to them and she wanted me to stay off. When she was about two arm's length away from me, she formed an x with her hands to tell me it was not safe to go there. I nodded in agreement but planned to venture out there at a later time because she clearly wasn't going to let me pass although I could've gone on if I really wanted.

"Anyway, one night… we all had a little too much to drink," the crew laughed as if they fondly remembered this.

"We lit lanterns to guide us around, but most of us were going in for the night as we had to go on another journey the following day. That's when one man from our crew went missing. Rye. Poor Rye…" He looked down and paused for a few moments. I wanted to ask him to continue but felt that this was a bad time to interrupt. He took a deep breath in and looked out at the waters as they clashed against the sides of the vessel.

"When I first noticed that he was missing, I grabbed a lantern and headed through the forest. There was a single glow coming from the pathway that led to the island. I followed it as a fly would be drawn to any glow under the night sky. When I reached the edge of the coast, just before the pathway... I was able to distinguish a figure that held one of the other lanterns. I called out to him and asked if he would come back. He was almost completely on the island by then. When he heard me, he turned around and waved at me as if nothing was wrong. As soon as he lifted his hand up in the wave, there was a monstrous beast that I cannot even begin to describe other than a black hole of darkness that slaughtered him so quickly that he didn't even have time to scream. I could hear his lantern that he held in his other hand fall to the ground as the glass crashed and flame went out. I still regret this deeply because no man should be left behind, but I ran as fast as I could away from the pathway and back towards the crew," he drank the remaining wine that was in his cup as if to drown his worries in that meager amount of liquid.

"Some still hear the beast's howls at the moon at times. While others… will see a faint glow coming from the island and I always wonder if that is Rye's spirit calling out for help," he said and walked away back into his cabin.

Docked

6

The multitude of nightmares that swarmed me each night from that story haunted me… even when I was awake, I thought about it. Sometimes, the dreams would just be pure darkness with a faint light glowing in the distance and as I tried to reach the light, the further away it became. No matter how fast I ran towards it, it seemed that much farther away. One morning, I woke up and found Jack fishing off the main deck. He was going about his business as if the Captain Oliver's story was just a myth.

"Hey, Jack… do you remember where you were when Rye was last seen?" I asked. If he boarded the ship since he was a young child, he would've surely been present at the time that Rye was taken.

"Just off the Northeast coast of America. Beautiful town actually and we will be heading there shortly to export some goods," he answered and continued pulling in the fishing line.

Part of me wanted to go to this island, but then the other side knew better. Whenever we would venture to America in order to drop off goods, I would always look out to see if there were any nearby islands. I dare not ask Captain Oliver as it was a bad memory of his. We had frequently visited the Northeast as new businesses were just starting and required many imports from the other countries. Several countries fought over the new land, but I was just glad not to be a part of that unending war. Captain Oliver was good to us in that if we got all of our work done, instead of heading back out to sea — he would allow us to spend the night to drink and relax in whatever town we happened to be in. This was one of those times.

Jack had turned into a bit of a wingman as he tried to teach me the ways with the ladies since I was now twenty-three.

"It's time we find a nice woman for you but be careful because there are some that will sneak their sticky fingers into your pockets and rid you of all your coin," he said as I nodded. I bet most women were like that. The sun was just setting and I followed him into a restaurant, which was quite different from what I was used to.

"We're in the wrong place, no? Where's the bar?" I asked. He tilted his head slightly as if to silently say 'this way,' as I followed. I was not dressed well enough to be at a restaurant to dine in. In fact, I didn't even have any clothes that I could've worn to a nice place out because I had never done that in my life. We walked past elegant women that were draped over their men's arms. Families sat with one another and looked unhappy as can be even though they were together at least. Finally, we came to the back of the restaurant to find the bar, which was mostly full of other men, one of which laid over a table and was sound asleep. He still held a glass cup in his hand as it tipped, letting the few drops that it still contained out onto the floor. He may have had too much to drink...

"Well, what do you think?" Jack asked as I sat on the wooden stool beside him. This part of the restaurant was much quieter despite it being the bar, but large crowds of families and other guests swarmed the main restaurant area. I was glad to not be on that side, but honestly would've much rather have taken my rum over to the ship to drink in my solitude. Jack was more of the social drinker than I.

"At first I thought we were in the wrong place but would've never known that they had this back here," I said. The bartender came over, interrupting our conversation.

"What would you like?" He asked.

"I'm easy. I'll take rum; he'll have the same," he said as he carried on the conversation with the bartender. I took this time to stare out at the wealthy families in the restaurant wondering what life was like for them. It looked awfully lavish and comfortable, but then there was the negative side in that they likely couldn't get a moment to themselves and had a high reputation to uphold at every second. I shuddered at the thought of being born into that. Times were hard for our family and the constant rumble of my stomach even after I ate dinner became a sound that I had grown used to. The women wore puffy dresses as the men wore layer upon layer with velvet coats atop what they were already wearing. They must have all been sweating. I looked down at my own ensemble which was carelessly thrown together as it was something I wore every day. Black slacks and a loose white shirt that had two buttons at the top. The uppermost clasp had fallen off and the only one that remained barely held on by a thread. The shirt came down just below my elbows and exposed half of my arms that had tanned from being out on the boat, under the hot beating sun each day.

My attention drew back up to the guests at the restaurant again when I heard the gentlest laughter that was one of the most beautiful melodies I heard my entire life. It was similar to that of a bird's chirp in spring as flowers bloomed and life came out from the still that used to be winter. The green stalks of grass that would gently grow out of the grounds, resembling nature's everlasting ways. Although it was not loud, I could just faintly hear it. Quiet enough that you could almost miss it but soothing to the ears and made you want to hear more of it. I followed the sound with my eyes as I surveyed the room. When I heard it again, I looked over at the far-right corner and noticed a woman sitting beside some other women at a table. It was odd, but there weren't any men at this table as there had been at the others. She wore an emerald dress that had white lace trailing up the middle to her chest. Her sleeves came down to her wrists and unlike the other women, this dress was not as puffy looking. Her wavy brown hair came down against her breasts, but when she turned her head I had noticed that half of her hair was up in a small bun held together by a gold clasp. I had almost hoped that someone would make her laugh again so that I could hear that music that struck me to my core, but instead she turned back towards her friend and met my gaze. At this point, I looked away and back at Jack, embarrassed. Someone of her reputation could never be caught with a man like me — without much to his name. Women who came from wealthy families usually married even wealthier noblemen. In any case, there were often arranged marriages to adhere to that rule. Jack nudged me hard in my side with his elbow as he seemed to catch what happened.

"Go over there," he joked. I laughed out loud at this advice as it would've likely gotten me killed. First off, the lady was far too delightful to have not already been taken by a nobleman. Secondly, everyone would surely laugh at a poor man like me attempting to woo a lady of that status.

"Yeah right, you'll have one less crew mate to report back with and would have to explain my absence to Cap't." The whole scenario played through my mind. I would go up to her and not be able to even get a word out of my mouth while all of her friends laughed at me. The second scenario would be that I'd get some words out, but my jaw would quickly meet the fist of some nobleman that had already snatched her up. Either way, Jack would still have a story to tell the other guys on the vessel. There wouldn't be an escape either once on the ship as they would all tease and taunt me and I'd have nowhere to run. I decided in my mind that I wasn't going to give them a story to talk about. Just as I was about to head back to the vessel, the crowds silenced. Looking out towards the far end of the room, a pair of musicians swept their attention as well as my own. One pulled out a light brown lute that looked to be carefully carved, likely by the musician's own hands. The other brought out a violin that appeared to be much older, but well-kept. It was likely passed down to him and kept through generations. Wasting no time, they began playing their instruments together in an uplifting tone.

It reminded me much of the fiddle that Patch used when we were young and I couldn't seem to help my foot from tapping against the ground to the melody. This English country dance was surely contagious and it was no wonder it made it all the way to America. Both musicians moved around back and forth to their own music. Some of the crowds stayed seated while others stood up and headed towards the center of the room to dance about. I looked over towards Sarah's table and saw that she wasn't there.

"A dance won't hurt, lad," Jack suggested. It was true, too. Even if she was taken by a suitor, people often switched partners with everyone that was dancing.

"What have I got to lose; we'll be out of here tomorrow…" I shrugged my shoulders and stood up, heading towards the center of the room as the others just had. I was surely the odd one out being that I wasn't dressed as elegantly as the others, but it was unlikely that they would see me after today anyways. I could make a complete fool of myself for all I wanted. Surprisingly, a woman with blonde hair and pale white skin reached for my hands right away and I bowed at her as she curtsied in return. We danced about the room weaving in and out of the other pairs. Attempting not to be rude, I glanced at her every so often, but also searched for the woman that caught my eye earlier. When our arms that had clung together were no longer touching, she moved onto another man while I wrapped my arm around the next woman. She had brown hair but was still not the one. After dancing with a few more women, I had given up and was about to turn back to tell Jack I was leaving and had no luck. Just as I began to walk away, I felt a gentle tap on my back and turned around to find the woman that I had been looking for all along, standing there in her emerald dress. She smiled and curtsied towards me while I tried to regain my composure and bow. As I wobbled forward a bit, she chuckled then wrapped her arm around mine as we turned in a circle to dance then whirled the other way. When she moved her arm away from mine, I knew that meant we must find new partners. Rather than switching people, I wrapped my arm around hers again and moved to another spot in the room. The blonde woman that I was supposed to dance with next squinted her eyes at me as if she had been looking forward to our dance. I shrugged it off because there was no one I'd rather be dancing with than the woman that I had in my arm. I moved my hand down to hold hers and held it up high so that I could twirl her. The bottoms of her dress flowed up as she went in a circle and her flowery perfume sent me into a daze. The musicians concluded their song and the others just looked over at us. An elegant woman of high status with a poor ship mate who scrubbed floors for a living. It was a sight that could catch anyone's eye. At that, she curtsied and I failed to bow as I just stood there in complete shock. One of the male suitors that was also dancing came around and wrapped his arm around her, pulling her away. She looked over her shoulder at me, eyebrows creased up in concern. I was right to think that she was already taken. Although when we danced she wore no ring, it was certain that she would be proposed to at any moment. I walked over to Jack and saw that he caught the entire exchange.

"I'll see you back at the ship, ok? I'm going to turn in for the night," it almost frustrated me that she was so close yet completely out of my reach. I had never met a woman who had mesmerized me so much and so quickly as she had. The fact that I didn't even know her name bothered me even more. This was something that I had to push to the back of my mind as I would be off tomorrow anyway in the ship to sail far away from her, likely never to see her again. I chose to go out the door farthest from her as not to catch her eyes again. As if my wishes had been granted, I heard the laughter again as I headed out and I had no choice but to look over in her direction. She raised her glass with the other girls and they clanged them together. The women at her table were looking at each other, but her eyes stared straight at me seeming to stare straight into my soul. I felt that she could see right through me. The man that had taken her away from me was in the table adjacent to hers, but they weren't talking at all. As I broke my gaze from hers, I rushed out the door, hoping her suitor didn't come after me to leave my body dead in an alleyway.

While we were in the bar, the sun had gone down and all was dark except for a few lit torches around each block. Laughter from each street blared out as I walked past a few drunken sailors trying to find their way home which was a common night for most towns — even back home at Port Glasgow. Continuing towards the ship, I ventured into even worse areas where the homeless lurked the streets and preyed upon people for any bit of coin that they could steal. It didn't scare me much since we would practice for things like this on the ship.

Sometimes, the guys would wrestle one another and it really did help prepare us for scenarios on land where people might attack us.

"Pretty lady behind you…" one said as he called over to me and started walking my way. I looked over my shoulder and saw the lady from the restaurant that had caught my eye. It practically stunned me.

Was this a dream?

Lady Sarah

7

"What are you doing here?" I asked and ran over towards the woman from the bar, putting an arm around her waist. I tried my best to deter her from the bad parts of town and headed in the opposite direction. Under normal circumstances, I would not have put my hands around a lady, but it wasn't safe for her to be walking around alone. Especially here.

"You were going to leave without even saying hi?" She asked, seemingly ignorant to her whereabouts.

"This is a bad place to be, especially at night. It's no place for a lady like you. Besides, your suitor took you away before I could," I said, frustrated. The homeless man had somehow caught up to us and was cat-calling her from behind. I had ignored it at first, but as he drew closer and reached his hand towards her, I snapped, sending my fist against his jaw. He grunted and held his hands up to his face as an immediate response to the pain. I stood there for a moment to see if he was going to continue trying, but he glanced my way then slowly walked off. If that didn't scare away this lady then I don't know what would.

I looked back at her, embarrassed at the monster that I had become in that split second. The sea had certainly made me rough around the edges, but there was still a tenderness deep within me. I could feel it when I looked into her brown eyes, which was right now. They sparkled in the moonlight, sending me into a trance-like state, unable to look away until she turned towards me. She grasped my chin in her delicate hand.

"Thank you for saving me....what's your name?" She paused, expecting an answer in return. Part of me wanted to tell her who I was, but then the other side was unsure as this was all useless. There was nothing that would come of this but torture on my part for a woman that I couldn't be with.

"William...William Kidd. I'm from Scotland," I couldn't deny her that if it at least meant that she would give me her name in return.

"You have nice eyes, William. Did anyone ever tell you that? Oh, you can call me Sarah..." She noted. I thought about my mother who passed down her green eyes to me. They reminded me of the grasses that stood tall next to the bluebells in spring. A compliment of that nature warmed me as I was happy to carry on something of my mothers in this world.

"We ought to get you back, I don't want to impose upon your suitor," I said, leading her towards the restaurant again that we had both just been at.

"Suitor? What suitor?" She scoffed. I wondered who the man was that took her away.

"That man that took you away from me when we danced… Well, at least let me walk you back to where it's safe, ok?" I turned towards her again, expecting absolutely nothing in return. For some reason, I felt a great need to protect her and make sure that she was alright even though I barely knew her.

"Haha! Jacob?! He is my brother! This is hilarious. Yes, you can walk me home," she sighed. It was likely that she had this similar treatment all of her life and was tired of being treated as the porcelain doll in the glass box. But that's exactly who she was…

"Why did you follow me?" I asked the question that I was dying to ask since I first saw her following me.

"My life is redundant and boring… it is the same every single night and day. Similar looking noblemen pass by me and later ask for my hand, but I say no each and every time. Tonight, I had been out with the ladies to celebrate another's engagement and you had caught my eye. At first, you didn't see me, but then when we locked eyes I was sure that you had been looking my way, too," she admitted. Unlike most girls, she wasn't very shy. She got straight to the point. And I liked that.

"Well, you're lucky that I'm the guy you chose to follow. Don't go doing that again because not all of us are nice guys out here…" I warned and thought about some other men that I had met who wouldn't have asked to have her as their own. They would've just taken… taken whatever they wanted and left her in some alley to be had again and again. She clearly did not know the ways of the streets which was understandable from someone of her reputation and class.

"So, what do you do?" She asked. I didn't answer right away because I was trying to think of a more eloquent way of saying "shipmate," but couldn't find one.

"I work on Captain Oliver's ship and have since I was thirteen years of age. This life is pretty much all I've ever known and wanted to know," I admitted. It was nothing to be ashamed of but would've sounded a lot better if I was telling her that I was the captain of my own vessel.

"You mean, you've been out in the open sea? I've only been once when I was very young. My family traveled here from Europe to expand our fur business in this region. We are one of the biggest companies that the Northeast has right now as we're the main fur trade. The winters are rough here, which makes us have even more of a purpose for our business," she explained.

Her job seemed much more detailed and elegant than mine. It was likely one that she would be able to retire early from and hire maids as well as other workers to do her basic chores for her. Again, another thing that I could never imagine having in my life. We were two sides of the same coin in that we both had a curiosity that ran deep within us for what life was like on the other side. She shivered and I pulled her closer to my side as we walked together through the dimly lit streets.

"We leave tomorrow. Unfortunately, we don't stay long when we dock, but we come back after we haul exports from other countries onto the ship and bring them back here," I said, looking down. For the first time in my life, I actually wanted to stay on land for just a while longer than I had planned to, so that I could at least get to know this lady more. She led me down streets that I hadn't traveled before as we would've surely been to the restaurant by then if we just kept walking straight. As I was so immersed in her presence, I hadn't noticed the change.

"So, you say you will be coming back… then I'll be seeing you again," she grasped her hand around my forearm and steered me down a cobblestone path that was carefully lit with torches going along the entirety of the way. At the end was a house, but a little closer stood a horse stable and small barn. She veered me over to the right to head towards the small barn.

"Is this your house?" I asked, stupidly. It seemed as though I was asking if she lived in a barn, but I more-so meant to ask if she lived in the house at the end of the cobblestone path.

"You've got nowhere to be tonight, so you could stay in the barn if you want. I bet it's better and warmer than that ship," she ignored my question. This struck me. How was this woman still alive if she was comfortable asking a stranger to stay near her home? Not to mention the fact that she was comfortable walking with me at night and led me back to her home...? Absurd... So absurdly beautiful and innocent... Jack had last seen me leave the bar without anyone and I wouldn't return to the ship, but this was a common thing for the crew to do when we stayed on land for a night. It was doubtful that they would ask questions unless I hadn't returned by our departure the following day.

"I don't want to impose..." I felt awkward to say the least as it should have been me providing for her, but instead she was taking care of me in a motherly way that I had not known for a very long time. The cool breeze sent her hair back over her shoulder and a flowery perfume filled the air. She smiled back at me and we continued walking towards the barn.

As I looked towards the barn, I saw an opening in between a few trees to its right. Through the gap, I could see the ocean but also a bit of land beyond that. It looked as though there was an island out there.

"What's that over there?" I asked, gesturing towards the island, hoping that she saw what I did as well.

"Oh, that is the forbidden island. We do not venture out there...after that captain...oh, your captain, Captain Oliver lost one of his crew mates years ago to the beast that is rumored to live there," she said and continued walking as if that was a normal story to share with just about anyone. She seemed to notice that I had still been staring out at the island.

"Don't you even think about it..." her tone grew stern.

"Well, that would be a good place to bury treasure since everyone is too scared to set foot on it… just saying…" I noted, lightening the mood. She giggled as we finally approached the barn.

Upon entering, she picked up a lantern that had been pre-lit and walked towards the stable. A horse poked its head through a small fence that kept it confined to one area.

"This is Melody," she rubbed the area in between the horse's eyes again and again. "Come, she doesn't bite." I walked over towards the horse that had quite the ironic name as that is what I had first thought of when I heard Sarah's laughter.

"Hey, sweet girl," I said in a feminine voice. For some reason, animals liked when I used this tone with them. I remembered the cats in Scotland that would follow me home - they would let me pet them if I used a lighter tone. Sarah giggled and handed me a brush to stroke Melody with.

"You can stay here tonight, it's nice and warm. And Melody promises not to bother you… too much," she said as she walked over to the other side of the barn and grabbed a few blankets to lay out on the hay.

"You really don't have to," I said. This was way more than I had asked… well, I hadn't even asked in the first place.

"I could tell you were a nice guy from the start. There's just something about you… I don't know. But thank you for not leaving me for dead in an alley, this is your repayment," she said. I walked over towards her and reached for both of her hands.

"I may not know much about you, but I am so glad that I met you," I could feel my cheeks becoming warm and if it weren't for the glowing lantern in the room, I would've been able to conceal the embarrassment in my face.

"Thank you, have a good night…Sarah," I hugged her body close to mine. In that moment, we were two pieces of the same puzzle that had finally found one another. The soft velvet of her emerald dress had become clouds underneath my fingertips and every breath of air sent my head into a flowery daze.

Darkness

8

A blanket of darkness encapsulated all that surrounded. Sarah had taken the lantern out with her when she left to go back to the main house. Gradually, the glow from the wick dimmed until it disappeared completely. All was still except for Melody's slow movements every now and then. For some odd reason, the ship was much more comfortable than where I lay in the barn. Prickly pieces of hay kept poking my body in every which way, causing me to readjust again and again. At one point, I even put the blanket down over the hay and wrapped myself in it.

What am I doing here?

If anyone in her family found me, I would surely be turned in as an intruder and may not even make the departure tomorrow with the rest of my crew... but surely they would have to wait for me... or maybe not. Who knows? I got up and used the small sliver of moonlight that shone in through the window of the barn to put the blanket as it originally was. It would look as though I had never even entered the barn. Melody whinnied, causing me to jump and I felt as though my heart stopped.

"Shh, shh..." I attempted to calm her, but that only seemed to startle her all the more. She backed up in the barn and came forward as far as she could without walking into the fencing that surrounded her stable. I had to keep her quiet or someone may come out to see what the ruckus was. At first, I hesitated to touch her, but then I met her smooth brown fur with my fingertips and stroked up.

"It's ok girl, you're in a good place," I said calmly as she settled down and stopped pacing back and forth. I had seen horses back in Scotland when I was just a child, but never got the chance to be as close to one as I now was. Nevertheless, I didn't quite know how to act near one and ensure that I wasn't startling them. This seemed to be doing the trick though. She tipped her head forward as if to ask for more and I gave in, stroking my hands between her black eyes and over the top of her head.

"You be good, sweet girl." With that, I turned around and headed out the way that I had come. It was pointless to stay here when nothing would come of Sarah and I. Delaying its inevitable demise would only torture me all the more. The sliding door was shut, but I gently moved it little by little as to not draw too much attention my way. I could see several stars in the night sky as the light from the full moon beamed down on the land surrounding me. If it had been a cloudy night, I would've likely had no idea where I was headed. Waves swooshed in the distance and gave me a clear direction for if reached the waters, it would only be a short time until I saw Captain Oliver's vessel. I could picture exactly how the calming swish of the waves looked without seeing them right in front of me. The water would come in on the coarse sands of the coast, covering shells that had been previously exposed. In the next few seconds, they would recede again. This repetitive dance was one of my favorites and just thinking about it caused me a calm that nothing else in the world had... until Sarah. She was a true breath of fresh air and a whirlwind all in one. Unlike the others, she was full of spontaneity and could surely keep one on their toes. The thought of her deep brown eyes underneath the moonlight... and how she felt in my arms... I had flings with other women whenever we'd dock, but this was no fling if only given the chance, which was very unlikely.

The cobblestone path was my only guide back towards the main streets from her home. It wasn't far but felt as though I had been walking forever and my torn shoes didn't make it any easier. When I came about halfway down the path that led to Sarah's home, a distinct light blared just above the tall grasses. I turned towards it and followed, wondering where it was coming from. As I drew closer, the light grew in size until I came up to the coast and couldn't walk any longer. The light remained but was on an island in the distance. It looked as though it was shaking left and right or perhaps it was just my tipsy state from the bar earlier. I did have a bit to drink but was usually able to tolerate more than what I had. As the glow from the island became easier to distinguish, a sudden yelp came from that direction. At the same time, the light crashed down - leaving nothing but the darkness once again, encapsulating all. It could've just been a drunken fool, lost and homeless. Shaking my head at the time I had wasted, I turned away and began walking back until my ears picked up an even more frightening sound. A high-pitched screech blared through my ears followed by the howl of a wolf-like creature. I turned around to look back at where it was coming from to find a beast that did not resemble a human in any way on the coast of that island. Although it had been on its hind legs, it had antlers protruding from its head while its back was arched. In the next moment, the beast seemed to turn towards me as if it was going to walk my way. I hesitated, not knowing where to turn. When I was just about to run in the opposite direction, the beast ran back towards the center of the island, out of view. Whoever had been holding the lantern was definitely mangled to the point that they no longer existed. Captain Oliver… his story must've been true. I began running in the opposite direction, back into town. After constantly looking back again and again to ensure that I wasn't being followed, I ran directly into someone and fell over them. They let out a painful moan as I lay on top of them. Lifting myself up, brown eyes beamed up at me, but her expression was much different than it had been before. Her eyebrows furrowed in and lips creased together in a pout.

"I'm so sorry, oh my god, are you ok?" I was still laying over her but lifted myself up so that I wasn't completely crushing her.

"Where are you going?" She groaned. A slight shadow from the trees drifted across her pale-white face. The fact that I had to come up with some reason as to why I was leaving without even saying goodbye was nerve-wrecking. If only I could find some way to escape having to answer her, then I wouldn't have to worry about it. There she lay underneath me, my heart pounding as I'm sure hers was too. The only difference was that my heart was pounding from what I had just seen on the island. As if it couldn't thump any harder, she made it speed up all the more. I looked down at her rosy lips and long eyelashes that blinked several times trying to make sense of this.

Suddenly, the loud growl that I heard earlier came again and rang through the once silent night sky. Sarah's eyes bulged open right into mine and with that, I stood up and took her hand in my own as we ran back to the barn together. Nearly tripping over roots from trees that poked out of the ground, we finally made it back.

"What was that?!" She was spooked and it surprised me that she hadn't heard the screams of the beast earlier.

"It is some creature on the island," I slid the wooden door open as the horse whinnied and stomped in its stable, clearly hearing the commotion.

"Are we safe here?" She questioned me and suddenly, I felt a great responsibility over her. Sarah rushed in and upon closing the door, I felt a warm presence wrap around me from behind. She must've come looking for me at the barn because the lantern within was lit in the corner of the room. I could see her glowing face, a light in the darkness. Although the horse continued stomping its hooves, Sarah took my face in her hands as she did before and I couldn't help myself as I put my own behind her head and pushed her into me, locking her lips with my own. She softly pressed into my chapped lips, moving back for air and pressing into me again and again. At first, our playful kisses were short pecks but they eventually turned into more… much more. When she pulled back one of the times, I could feel her teeth nibble my bottom lip. As her nibbles became harder, I wrapped my arms around her back and pushed her against the wall of the barn, pressing my body against hers as to share warmth. What once was a cool spring night turned scorching.

"I don't…know you," she said in between kisses.

"Then why don't you get to," I pulled back and looked at her deep in her eyes. I wanted to know everything about her. What did she do each day, where did she like to go, what was her favorite food to eat, her morning routine, her thoughts before she went to sleep each night…something about her caught my eye the instant I entered that restaurant. And against any other lady in the room, she was the one that I saw, a calm in the storm. A breath of fresh air. She was the transparency in the fog that I had looked for and it had taken the longest time, but I could finally see clearly.

"You leave tomorrow," she reminded me and I had never thought that I would find someone worth staying on land for. Never in a million years.

"I will come back for you," I reassured her. Someone like her was worth waiting for and if it meant that I had to write letters from afar in order to keep her in my life in any way, then I would.

Written Promise

9

Waves of orange and yellow peeked in through the window of the barn. This time, I wasn't in a rush to watch the sunrise as I had the most gorgeous woman I had ever laid eyes on sleeping beside me. Sometime during the night, she had taken the entire blanket off my body and wrapped it around herself. At one point, I woke up and noticed what she had done. Laughing quietly to myself, I pulled her closer in a careful embrace so as not to wake her. Rosy lips pressed together; her eyes were shut and the entirety of her face was still. Her motionless expressions made it feel as though the entire world had stopped so that I could stare a while longer. Long, dark eyelashes pressed down against the tops of her glowing cheeks. Hiding out in the barn and being her special servant had crossed my mind, but it wasn't good for someone like me - being out at sea seemed to keep me out of trouble...trouble on land anyway.

I walked up to Melody to pet her before leaving and she whinnied, waking Sarah on cue. She rolled over and reached both arms out to stretch then locked eyes with me. The shocked look on her face made me feel like I had done something terribly wrong. Perhaps she wanted me to leave sooner?

"You know…you're the first person who hasn't tried to jump forward with me," she said, sleepily. I walked towards her and extended my hand out to help her up.

"And same for you, madame," I retorted back, unable to keep myself from grinning. She smiled in return and the joy on her face soon fell into a frown. I wished that I could always see that smile, but knew it was sure to come again the next time we docked in the Northeast.

"You have to leave…" she stated. This was the first time that I had to be reminded of setting sail again for I usually counted the minutes until the next voyage. Now, I had a feeling that I would be doing the exact opposite. I looked down at my feet, contemplating the idea of sneaking her in on the ship with me.

"Think I could fit you in my pocket?" I joked, trying to lighten the mood. She laughed and pushed my chest playfully. I just put out my hands as if to ask 'what' in all seriousness. Bringing her to my hometown of Port Glasgow would've meant everything to me. I could've even shown her to mother and she wouldn't even know what to say. A while ago, I told mother that I wouldn't be finding a lady to marry, but the exact opposite happened and now I was trapped by my need to be two places at once. While I had to go back on the ship, I also wanted to be there for Sarah. It was still far too unlikely because of our clashing reputations. But one could dream… We would walk by the docks and up over the hills towards my home. It was small and I hadn't grown up with much, but I would've taken that any day over a cold, unwelcoming mansion where I had to look over my shoulders at all times. I'd pick some bluebells for her and mother. They'd put them together by the window as mother always would whenever I brought them home.

The village that I was from enjoyed nights together after a long week. Everyone would bring some type of food and we'd all feast around the fire, telling stories. Patch's family knew how to play the fiddle and passed it down to him so he'd often play, too. Although most of us were dirt poor, we still knew how to have a good time.

"I'll at least walk you to your ship, ok? Let me go into the house and freshen up. I'll be back in ten," she woke me out of my daze. The daydream that I never wanted to end would've had to continue at another time.

"Sure," I replied. For some reason, she wasn't going anywhere and instead stood right there, frozen in front of me then smirked.

"No running off anywhere, got it?" Her bossy tone made me want to laugh. I felt like I was a child again and had just gotten into trouble with Mrs. Sarabella for the umpteenth time. She couldn't stand it either when I would just smile at her no matter how much trouble I was in. If the crew mates caught sight of this, they would've never let me live it down. It would be all everyone talked about each night. Thankfully, they weren't there. I nodded in agreement. I had tried running off and that didn't work out too well.

When she walked off, I went back to petting the smooth fur on Melody's head. She reminded me of the cats that would follow me home from school back in

Scotland. There were plenty of cats there that needed homes and food. It was nice to have an animal by your side or even to come to at the end of the day. They didn't pass judgement on you and loved unconditionally. Out of all the times I caused trouble in Port Glasgow, I was sure that I must've fit right in with the cats of town who had been known for stealing the local merchants' food and playing with supplies.

"Hey there, I've seen you've made acquaintances with Melody… she seems to like you," she noted as Melody whinnied in response. Sarah came up beside me and gave me a brush to comb Melody's fur properly. She had a beige dress on that went down to the ground, covering her feet. It was much more casual than the emerald one that she had on at the restaurant, but still accentuated every bit of her and brought even more light to the day. It didn't take long for me to stop what I was doing so that I could put my arm around her once again.

"Shall we?" I asked and she smiled, but I could tell deep down that it was but a mere mask. Maybe telling her that I was literate and would be able to send letters to her during my travels would brighten her mood… but I would save that for our last goodbye.

We walked along the cobblestone and goosebumps covered my skin in fear as I thought of what I had seen and heard the prior night. It all confirmed Captain Oliver's story of the beast that lurked on the forbidden island. Although the waters washed away perfectly to reveal a pathway, it was still off-limits to all due to the rumors. Except now, they were no longer rumors and the worst nightmares had turned into a horrifying reality. I held my arm around Sarah and pulled her closer. She could tell that I was tense and leaned into me, pecking my neck gently with her lips.

"Whatever you do, stay away from that island. Promise?" I stopped walking and looked into her eyes, not wanting to break my gaze until she agreed whole-heartedly. She gently pressed her palm to my cheek and leaned in for a kiss.

"It's sweet that you worry about me," she said, pulling back. She began to trudge forward but I wasn't budging until I heard her words.

"Please just promise. I can't be here to protect you," I assured her, regretfully. I'm not quite sure what good I was so far away from her, but hopefully the promise would mean something to her and she wouldn't go out there.

"I, Sarah, solemnly promise you, William Kidd, that I will never go out to that island," she firmly said. The formality in her voice caused me to shiver and she curtsied politely to close the promise that she made. I pulled her body against mine and wrapped my arms around her as if I would never see her again. When you're a crew mate with frequent voyages around the world, you never know if you will make it back. From the storms of the seas and battle zones that we muster our way through, I was unsure if I would ever be back. But that bit I must keep to myself. She moved away from me, still holding my dry, coarse hand in hers and we began walking again.

As we moved away from her house and down through the village, we finally came to the docks. With high tide, the waters had pushed up close to the very edge of the floorboards that led out to each docked boat. I could see Jack already on the vessel. He peered out at us from afar and then waved when he recognized that it was me beside the lady. I decided not to invite her onto the ship as the men could be savages when it came to ladies and the last thing I needed was to see their eyes feasting on her appearance. Instead, I stopped cold in my tracks and took her face in my hands as she had done to me before. Her deep brown eyes flickered in the sunlight as small black lines crept through each bit of light brown. They had a softer look to them than they had the previous night, but also a contagious sense of sadness.

"I will write to you," I revealed. Her eyebrows shot up in surprise.

"You can write?" She asked. "Err, sorry. I'm not trying to say that you don't know how…uh.." she tripped over her own words, but I just smiled and pulled her close. I heard the yells of Jack and the crew from the ship as they called out my name and pulled out a piece of paper and quill that I kept in my satchel. She dipped the quill in the ink jar that I shakily held then scribbled over it. As she handed it back to me, I waved it in the air trying to let the ink dry.

"I will be in touch," I promised.

"I'll be looking out for your letter," she kissed me once on the cheek. My crew mates were still watching as I heard kissing sounds mocking me. I could feel my cheeks grow warm and full of color. With that, I ran over towards the ship and once I was beside Jack, I waved back at her as we pulled away from the docks.

"So that's where you were…" he said, grinning. "I didn't get that lucky." I knew exactly what he was thinking. And it wasn't like that… not one bit.

"We didn't do anything," I protested like a little boy that got his hands caught in a cookie jar.

"Sure William…sure," he said and walked off to help the crew release the sails.

The following day, I had been standing on the stern of the vessel, looking out at the sunrise. Waking with the rise of the day always planted new ideas in my mind. I shuffled back to the kitchen where I kept my satchel and took out the quill and paper. Once we made it to land, it would be quite difficult to find the time to write letters and before the sun went down, I planned to use its light. As I ran back up the steps, I carefully avoided the other men so that they wouldn't distract me by mocking my recent love. Taking the quill and dipping it into the ink, I set the paper on the side railing of the boat to attempt to write. Although the ship swayed back and forth in the sea, I was able to keep my hand somewhat steady enough so that it didn't all look like a child wrote it.

Dearest Sarah,

From the moment I laid eyes on you, I felt myself glued to the very sight of your contagious smile. Even when we were two strangers in a crowded room, your laughter brought me back home again when I thought I didn't even have a home anymore. The open seas are where I always wanted to be most until I met you and felt the warmth of your presence by my side. Now I realize that is where I always long to be. Two sides of one coin, we each make up for the nature of which the other doesn't have. Promise me that you will steer clear of the island and its horrific ways as I am not there to keep you safe.

Love,

William Kidd

No Sign

10

An undistinguishable aura surrounded the crew as something had been off the entire day. Cap't was in his quarters and no one had heard from him, but we figured he was just getting some much-needed rest. By sunset, Jack went into his cabin and found him asleep except it was not so typical for someone sleeping. The way that he described it to me:

"All was quiet and he had the usual glass bottle of whiskey. The glass that would normally be in his hand was on its side on the floor with the remaining liquid spilt out next to it. This was the first strange sign because captain would never leave anything in a glass, especially if it was his favorite whiskey. Letting it pour onto the floor would have been one of the worst sins to him." At that, Jack walked closer- trying not to disturb him, but at the same time ensuring that he was okay. The second sign that alerted him was the dormancy of his body aside from the rocking of the ship. There must have been a big wave that hit us because it rocked the ship far right and as a result, his body rolled, hitting the wall. There was no response from him whatsoever. No groan, murmur or words. Just the thud of his lifeless body. He went closer and rolled him onto his back. The disturbing details of what Jack saw made me feel that I was there too, as it haunted me and any time I would think of captain, I couldn't seem to escape from the horrifying image that clouded my mind.

His light blue eyes were stretched open to the point that you could see the entirety of the murky white that framed the color that had begun to gloss over. Rosy cheeks were now pale as every ounce of color had faded from his face. No longer full of life. It gently blended with his long, white hair that used to be dirty blonde when I had first met him many years before. When Jack blurted out captain's name, that's when everyone knew what was wrong. We never used his name. The alert of 'Oliver!' sent everyone into a panic as we huddled into his quarters. Each man tried to creep over the other to assess the situation. It had been twenty years that I was sailing with this crew and the captain served as a reminder of my father and my efforts to please him made me feel like I was pleasing my own father. When Jack and Harry carried his body out and laid him to rest at sea, I felt that I had lost another father in my life. In the same token, I was thankful to have the remainder of the crew. I remembered that night distinctly; we held a fire in honor of him. The crewmen shared stories of their rich memories with Captain Oliver. Some of these stories I had never heard before.

A few days passed and we had docked our ship. That's when everything changed. Another captain took over for our previous one and what had been a family to me changed immensely. Some of our crew was allowed to stay, but others had been replaced with French-English men and it was no longer predominantly a Scottish crew. As soon as he set foot on our ship, he announced his name as if he was worth his weight in gold.

"You can refer to me as Captain Jean Fantin," he beamed at the sound of his own voice. "Things will be a little different around here. No more time for games or playing around. You listen or you walk the plank," he firmly said as he checked out the crew by looking them up and down.

The scowl on his face showed that he wasn't impressed in the slightest. Jean... because I will never refer to him as Captain... was just about the shortest man on the ship besides some other kids that found refuge in setting sail and fleeing their homes in hopes for a better life. He was even shorter than Harry whom I nearly lined up against when I was just thirteen years of age. His ash-gray mustache curled up at the ends and prickles of hair stood up at the edges of his chin. His face was covered in dirt and he had long hair that matched his stringy mustache. The next thing that he did, none of us could have guessed..

Without warning, he took steady steps towards the captain's cabin and opened it. We hadn't entered since Captain Oliver's death. His cloak and other remnants were still in the cabin. On one side, the French-English men stood together, with their arms firmly crossed over their chests. Jack and I were some of the last few Scottish men that were left after the others had been replaced. It felt as though someone came into our home and was beginning to trash the place so much so that they may as well have lit the entirety of the ship on fire. I looked over at Jack in question as to what Jean must be doing in the cabin. He seemed to read my thoughts and shrugged his shoulders, unknowingly. In the next second, the wreckage that our home had now become was even worse than we could've imagined. Like a knife straight through the heart, Jean came out with Captain Oliver's deep-red cloak over his shoulders. It barely fit him and almost trailed down against the wooden deck. With his hands around his hips, he began pacing back and forth as if he was now officially captain just because he wore the cloak...

"Hey, that's Captain Oliver's!" One of the Scottish crewmen shouted out. In the next moment, Jean smiled deviously and pulled out a pistol from his belt. Without the slightest hesitation, he shot the man that he didn't even know point blank. His body hit the floorboard with a thud as blood pooled around him.

"What are you all waiting for? Get to work! We've got to set sail shortly, go go go! Oh and clean up that mess," he yelled out at everyone and then wandered back into the cabin. I stepped forward, wanting to barge in there after him and take his grimy fingers off the things that didn't belong to him. Jack's arm extended out and stopped me in my tracks. I looked over at him, furious. *I could settle this once and for all. Why would he stop me?*

Without saying any words, he tilted his head over to the right and I followed his gaze. The new crew mates. Of course. If I was going to do something to their 'captain' then they would likely not give me the time of day to explain and it would be over for me, too. I moved my head next to Jack's ear to whisper a solemn promise,

"He won't last very long," I walked off.

Days had passed as I spent every free moment plotting ways of which we could rid ourselves of Jean. Jack and I had come up with a plan of sneaking the key to his chambers so that we could stage his death. This plan was quite difficult because it meant that we had to ensure that no one would blame us.

I stared out at the crashing waves as the wind blew through my hair which was now down to my shoulders. Water splashed up the sides of the boat and receded back into the depths of the ocean. This dance went back and forth in an ongoing charade that was mesmerizing to watch. In the fore mast, I was farthest away from Jean and that was exactly where I wanted to be whenever I could because each day was proving more and more difficult for me to control myself. He seemed to see right through me as he caught on to my deep disliking of him. Because of this, he gave me one job that I had no interest in and that was to mop the deck floors atop of cooking for the crew, which I was already doing all along. Luckily, Jack and I were paired together. Jack would help fish while we were away at sea and I cooked up all the fish down below, not able to look out at the water as much. If I had known this, I would have surely stayed home in Scotland to work at some of the restaurants there. At times when I could get away, the fore ship was where I stayed. Leaning against the side, I stared out into the never-ending waters that I longed to journey in. Instead, we were forced to do a series of unimportant jobs here and there for wealthy noblemen. Jack walked up alongside me with a net full of fish. They sparkled in the sunlight and almost blinded me from looking at them as they flipped up and down, mouths gaping open to suck in the nonexistent water around them.

"See anything good out there?" he asked, hanging the net over the open waters. If what had previously been torture for the fish, this was pure hell. Not only were they unable to breathe because they didn't have access to water, but now they flopped above an open sea... still without reach. It reminded me much of myself. Here I was in the open sea yet still a prisoner to someone else's worthless commands.

"Always," I said and looked around us to ensure that no one was close enough to listen.

"Were you able to get a key to the cabin?" I whispered, still keeping watch around us in case someone decided to sneak up and bud into our conversation. In his other hand, he reached into his pocket and gently pulled up the tip of a key out of his pocket but dropped it back in so that no one would see. I nodded, confirming that I saw it.

"Good work," then I tapped him on the back a few times and took the net of fish from his hand. Jack and I had conspired for a long while about how we would get rid of Jean. Since we were on a ship, someone would surely have to brunt the blame. The best way to do this was to stage it, which was difficult but still seemed to be the only way without the blame shifting to us. The person had to be somewhat caught in the act so that it was believable. We had decided to frame one of the

Englishmen who was his righthand man. At night, Jean liked to get very drunk just as the other sailors did. Since he would stay in his quarters, his righthand man would often stay in there with him so that he had access to some of the best drinks. Due to this, he would often get far more drunk than the others. I had found a potent drink near the pantry that I used for my cooking supplies. It was sure to knock him out and if we could just get the gun or knife into his hands and then escape quick enough, it would look as though he did it accidentally having been so drunk. It would knock him so hard on his ass that he would barely notice what was going on before it was too late and already happened. This ought to be believable to him too because he would wake up with the worst headache he could ever imagine from the drink and not remember a thing. When told that he shot his gun incorrectly and it pierced through Jean's heart, that would be all he needed to hear before believing that he did kill Jean. It may not go completely according to plan, but we had to at least try. When Jean first came on the ship, he dropped one of our men like a fly without hesitation. With that, there would surely be more unless we were able to put a stop to it.

The following hours seemed to drag on as I held the rusted key in my hand that could change my life forever. While I fried up the fish for dinner later that day, all I could do was pace back and forth past the wine bottles that stood in front of the most potent drink that I could find. This had to be done so that Jack and I could get our lives back. It was the only way. As I paced back and forth, deciding whether or not I was actually going to follow through with the plan - the bubbles of hot oil snapped me out of my indecision. Rushing over to the stove, I managed to somehow trip over a small brick that had been randomly placed before the stove. I found myself on the floor, face down into the wooden floorboards that hadn't been mopped in far too long. Crumbs of food and other trash stuck to my darkened beard. I pushed myself back up so that I could get to the nearly overflowing pans of fish before it caused an even bigger mess. While standing, I saw that the fish was still salvageable and plated them up, looking at the key one last time before bringing dinner out for the crew.

Traitor in the Midst

11

No one seemed to mind the oily fish that I left in far longer than intended. My own mind seemed to get the best of me as it wandered to various places much of the time, one of which was a reoccurring daydream of Sarah as she lay sound asleep next to me in the barn. But ever since Jean boarded the ship, all I could picture in my mind was how I could get rid of him. After everyone received their plates, Jack and I leaned against the wooden railing of the ship's side, far from the captain's cabin. As twenty years had passed, Jack wasn't as fast as he had always been and his ragged hair was now mostly grey. The way that he leaned back against the side of the ship looked as though he was forcing all of his weight onto it. There was no way that I could have done this without him by my side the entire time. Hell, I would still be scrubbing dishes back home if it weren't for him. But was this much better than the job of a dishwasher? The open sea made it worth it without a doubt.

At first, we stood in silence and just stared out at the rest of the crew. A few of our old mates that were still kept on as crew were cleaning their plates off and helping so that I did not have as much to clean after. Remnants of food were tossed on the grounds causing vermin to have their feast after our own. We took one look at one another and realized that we had been looking at the same thing in disgust. If we could get rid of the part of the crew that Jean brought on, we would. Unfortunately, that was not in the cards for us. Jean alone would have to do.

"You still have it?" He broke the silence between us. I nodded, trying not to give off too much to the others. As I made my way down the steps and towards the kitchen, my palms suddenly felt sweaty and I was unsure I could actually carry out the mission that I previously intended on. Taking deep breaths, I tried to pretend this was a night like any other and poured several glasses of wine. In the tallest glass that had a slight blemish on the bottom, I used the potent drink and noted which glass it was in as not to make a mistake and give it to the wrong person. A brief hesitation caused me to pause for a few moments before heading back up with the tray of glasses. This would be the first time that I was in direct correlation with someone's death. Jean had been terrible to us from the start, including sending off several shipmates that had worked on this ship almost their entire lives. He threw them out as if they were old pieces of garbage. Most, if not all of them, didn't even have a home to go back to. I started back up towards the top deck, laughter bellowing in the salty air that surrounded us. I continued reassuring myself. This was just like any other night where I would bring up drinks after they all feasted like savages on the food that I made. It wasn't the first time that I had to put on a mask and act as everything was ok.

"Everyone, I've got your drinks!" They stayed put as I walked over and handed each a cup while putting a bottle in the middle of the group. They carried on talking as I kept walking towards the captain's cabin as that was usually where Jean stayed. Before heading in, I walked over to the edge of the ship and looked out over the water that had echoed the moon's bright reflection. Taking the potent glass with the blemish on the bottom, I threw it overboard and then turned around to continue walking into his quarters. The next sight that I walked in on was one that I wasn't exactly prepared for to say the least…

Before coming into his quarters, I would usually knock. But this time, I slowly opened the door and found him in the corner with his back faced towards the door. There was a large bag to his right that he was filling with items from the cabin. I hadn't the slightest idea as to what he was packing and with that… why he was packing in the first place.

"Want some wine?" I asked, continuing to walk towards him and beginning to pour a drink. His first mate wasn't in with him, but I already decided against poisoning anyone. It wasn't the right way. Jack would have to understand… surely he would as we could find another way.

"No, no, no. Get out of here," Jean exclaimed in a rushed tone. My curiosity peaked at this point. There was no way that I was getting out of the cabin without finding out what was going on.

"You need any help over there?" I continued, refusing to leave. Jean stood up and turned around, blocking whatever was behind him from my view. He put his hands on his hips and his face alone could have said a thousand words. Sweat streamed down the sides of his temples and cheeks that were now a deep shade of red. The only red that grew from embarrassment or anxiety.

"I said… I do not need your help. Now, scram!" He belittled me down to the same level as vermin as if I was of no value. The more he pushed me away, the more eager I was to stay and get to the bottom of whatever it was that he was doing. As Captain Oliver's close mate, I felt obligated to take a stand for what used to be his belongings and hard-earned fortunes. I treaded towards him in slow, lengthy strides as he took off his cloak and dropped it over the bag that he had been filling. When I was just about two arm's length away from him, he grew even more defensive and pulled out his gun.

"I swear, if you come any closer…" he threatened. I felt as though it was an empty threat even though he held the gun in front of me. There was a thing or two that I had learned from Captain Oliver before his passing and having sailed for twenty years with him, it was necessary for crew mates to learn how to take a stand as life was just as rough with other people as it could be on the open seas.

"What will you do?" I now crossed my arms over my chest showing that I wasn't scared. I towered over this small man and somehow, he was even smaller in personality there as he stood in front of me. He took out a bullet and loaded it down the muzzle, showing how serious he was at firing the musket. What I was about to do, I had to quickly and without delay as it would mean my life if he was actually sincere about his threat which he appeared to be. In an instant, I rushed towards him, ducking under the musket and pushed it out of his sweaty grasp, knocking it down to the ground where it went off. The bullet shot towards the roof of the cabin as a hole sent it through the top deck. In the next few seconds, we heard a scream and someone collapsing to the ground who must've been in the direct path of the bullet. I ignored this and wrestled Jean to the ground with little effort, looking around to see if I could find any sort of constraints so that I could bring him out to the main deck in one piece. I rolled him onto his front and pulled both of his arms back, grabbing a nearby rope that had been tangled and interwoven into itself as a giant pile of knots.

"What are you going to do, take the captain out onto the main deck and show what a traitor you are?" He asked.

"I haven't decided yet, but whatever you have in that bag can't be good for your reputation here. You're hiding something from us and I'm sure they won't like the sounds of it either," I said, unsure of whether or not I would actually find something worthy enough to show the crew. It was worth a shot, though. He didn't seem to like the sound of this as his previous tone had changed drastically.

"Wait, let's talk about this. Ok? What do you want? I'll double or… I'll even triple your coin. I'll give you a bonus, is that what you want?" He asked.

It sounded too desperate. I rushed to untangle the end of the rope so that I could at least constrain him while I checked the bag. Straddling his back as he squirmed this way and that, I finally managed to tie his hands together behind his back. The desperation in his body's convulses reminded me of the fish out of water that Jack would frequently catch. In an effort to ensure that he didn't escape, I tied his ankles and legs together as well with the same rope. He laid there on the floor, face on its side as he watched me get up and walk over to the bag that had been concealed by his... Captain Oliver's coat...

"Please, let's just talk about this," was his last futile attempt at a negotiation. A terrible one at that too... Mrs. Sarabella had been right about one thing all those years ago, I was indeed stubborn. As I picked up the coat, shining pieces of gold jewelry and coin beamed out from within the contents of the bag. The anger within me made me want to grab the musket and see if there was another bullet within so that I could end it for him. But an even worse demise was what the crew would possibly do with him.

"You… were… You were making a run for it with the coin?" I said, feeling as if steam was coming out of my ears.

"I was putting it away to keep it safe, that's all." A lie. I knew a lie when I heard one. He thought I was a fool.

"Oh, we'll see what the crew has to say about this…"

Blessed William

12

The knocks came suddenly and without warning. In the time that it took me to tie Jean up and find what he had been hiding, the crew had definitely noticed if not for the shot of the musket. They didn't wait for an answer and busted in by the piles. In sync, they looked over at Jean as he was still tied down to the floor, then up at me. What they saw could've definitely been taken the wrong way, but their eyes went to the bag beside me. Before I could open my mouth, Jean beat me to it.

"I was packing it away for safe keeping," he stammered, still squirming this way and that like a fish trying to escape back to its home. Idiot… if he had just kept his mouth closed, that may have saved him, but he pretty much gave himself away. At first, it felt as though I had been caught red handed and I was wondering how I would explain why I was in the captain's quarters let alone next to a bag of gold that could've been framed as my own. The crew looked over at him and then back at me when he stopped talking.

"I caught him acting suspicious when I was bringing the wine over to him and found that he was packing a bag of coin and other gold that Captain Oliver had earned. He was going to flee sometime in the night when we arrived back in the Northeast," I put the pieces to the puzzle together in my mind as I explained it to them. It all made sense now.

Harry, who used to be Captain Oliver's righthand mate, stepped out before the crowd of other crew mates. He dabbed a damp cloth to his forehead to wipe the sweat away, not knowing what to expect. The worried look in his eyes told me that there was far more on his mind than just that, though.

"It seems to me that you… Jean, are a traitor. And you know what we do with traitors…" he walked over towards me and patted my shoulder twice as if I was a dog and had done a good job.

"We will get back to you, Jean. There is another matter that we need to deal with that is of urgency on the top deck," he said and signaled some of the crew mates to stay with Jean.

"What happened?" I asked. The concern in Harry's face alarmed me as it had usually been flushed red from his many drunken nights. But now, he was stern and serious — the only other time I saw him as rigid was when we found Captain Oliver dead in his chambers.

"Come with me," he led me towards the top deck. We went up above the stern of the ship and saw a frail man lying on his side. The mixture of gray and light brown hairs covered the back of his head as he was turned away from us. From the large tunic that covered his torso along with his ragged, but wavy hair, I could tell that it was him. I rushed over to his side before Harry could even begin to explain what happened. His strained breaths weakened by the minute as he held his arm to his chest, in pain.

"What happened, Jack??" I asked. For some reason I couldn't put two and two together. At the same time that I wanted to take care of him, I also wanted more than anything to tell him what I had found. It hadn't quite clicked how Jack became injured as I was wrapped up in dozens of thoughts about what to do next. I decided against telling him that we finally found a way to get rid of Jean even though it may have helped him feel better.

"You have been like a son to me," he said through uneven breaths. The words that escaped his lips had sucked out most of the energy that remained within him. Harry walked over and knelt down beside the two of us.

"Whoever shot the musket aimed it at the roof of the cabin, hitting Jack right in the chest. I'm surprised that he's still breathing at all. I think he waited for you," Harry noted. I almost felt that it was my fault and the feelings of guilt swarmed around me that I had buried deep down hoping they would never reappear. This time, there was no dirt to dig a hole in and hide. I was out in the open as the crew stood behind me watching as if this was some kind of performance. A performance of humility and heartbreak was all this was. If only they could just all walk away…

I turned my attention to Jack again. His eyelids were slowly closing and reopening. I didn't know what to say to him. I needed to explain what happened but wasn't sure if that really even mattered now.

"Jack, I lost my father at a very young age and you have been like a father to me and have shown me family when I thought I had lost most of them. I am sorry that I couldn't protect you," I said feeling the tears stream down my cheeks. Normally, I wouldn't want anyone to see me like this. But at this point, I didn't care much. I pressed my body down on his as if to shield him from the brutal world and wrapped my arms around his nearly lifeless body in a hug. Closing my eyes, I planned to stay there until people yanked me away. There was no energy in me to even stand myself up. Surely they would all grow bored after a while and clear out.

"There is only one thing to do now," Harry croaked. "William Kidd must take Jean's place as Captain and lead us back to the Northeast." This alarming news broke me from my depressions and when I looked up at Harry, the entire crew still stood there, watching.

"All those in favor of Captain Kidd, say aye," Harry continued. What followed struck Jack and I alike as his eyes were now open, too, holding onto the last few breaths that he had.

"Aye," the crew said in its fullness and no one else would've been able to hear, but Jack too whispered out his answer in agreement. My gaze switched from the crew to Jack again as a painful tranquility surrounded us in silence. His lips trembled as he strained to speak through the pain and exhaustion.

"You will make a good captain, I always knew you would," he said and closed his eyes with a smile on his face - one last confirmation that it was, in fact, okay. Although he tried to assure me that I was meant for that position, I couldn't help but feel that I had just landed in it by mere luck and chance. I had done nothing to truly deserve it and now I had an entire crew to lead. The time of being a troublemaker had passed long ago as I would now captain this vessel. Mrs. Sarabella's words etched into my mind as my thoughts circled one memory in class. We spoke of the letter written to the Corinthians in the Bible:

'Corinthians 5:7-12 You must remove the old yeast of sin so that you will be entirely pure. Then you will be like a new batch of dough without any yeast, as indeed I know you actually are.'

I stood up tall, knowing exactly what had to be done. This was a time that had been coming for a while. Although change is difficult for everyone, sometimes it is necessary in order to achieve your dreams. One may find comfort in the perpetual routines of life, but are they truly happy when comfortable? Or is it just the mere thought and mirage of relief that deceives us into thinking that we have obtained happiness? If mother had taught me anything as a young child, happiness is not something that one can obtain… but instead, it is the acceptance of oneself as a complete being.

"This new ship will be 'Blessed William' and we will set for the Northeast of America to arrive in the morning's light. You all deserve a day off. When we dock, we will take the day and night to celebrate in town. The following day, it'll be back to work," I firmly said. They all seemed to like the idea as some gathered the wine bottles and Harry handed me a glass. One of the others poured wine in the glass and we all lifted our glasses up in unison,

THE CURSED VESSEL

"To Captain Kidd!! Blessed William we sail!!"

Deserved

13

The bittersweet day was coming to an end and for the first time in my life on the ship, I felt as though I had a purpose and duty. If not for myself, I needed to do this in both Jack and my father's memories. After Jack took his last few breaths and I had officially been named "Captain," I walked down to the captain's cabin again to deal with Jean. Instead of aiming my anger at myself, it was instead on him. If it weren't for his suspicious acts then Jack would have still been alive. I walked in to find that he still lay on the ground and the crew mates had roughed him up a bit already. One of his eyes was bruised and swollen shut in black and purple crusted shades while he laid on his side in pain, moaning and groaning. I had no sympathy but had never been much of a talker - instead, I would much rather show what I was going to do. In this case, I needed the help of my crew, though.

"Untie him and bring him to the top floor," I said, walking back out of the cabin. If I had my way, I wouldn't take another look at the traitor. They must've followed my orders because all I heard behind me was scampering and shoving as Jean protested that he was innocent. On the main deck, there were wooden rowboats attached to the sides of the ship. One of them would have to be sacrificed, but it would be well worth it…

"You want to send him out on a boat?" Harry questioned, perplexed. I turned to him, breaking my gaze.

"You'll see," I said, neglecting to answer his previous question. At first glance when I initially met Harry, I hadn't thought much of him except for the fact that he was a lazy fool… but after this - I realized how loyal he truly was to his crew.

"I knew he was up to something, but just couldn't seem to catch him in the act. He must've done this on the other ships that he captained, too," he said. Two crew mates held Jean by each of his arms, careful not to let him loose. He was too bruised up to fight back much and clearly couldn't walk on his own.

"What do you want us to do with him, Captain?" they asked. Jean seemed to snap out of the daze that he had just been in as he started chuckling.

"Captain?! Did I wake up somewhere else entirely?!" He continued laughing hysterically, tears coming from his eyes as they streamed down his dirty, bruised cheeks. I smiled at him and drank half a jug of water then slipped it on the paddle boat.

"Here's your boat," I said, ignoring his questions.

"What do you mean?" He asked, shockingly serious in tone now. His once smug face no longer had the same look to it anymore and this was likely the first time I saw him scared out of his boots.

"This is far more than you deserve. If we brought you back to land with us, it would be sure death anyway. Take the water and boat. Wherever you end up, if you do end up anywhere… don't ever show your face to this crew again," I grabbed his arm forward as the other men helped on Jean's other side. Despite the many weak pushes and pulls in protest, we lifted him and placed him in the paddle boat.

"Come on, William… you know me. I didn't mean any harm. I'll make you my first mate if you just let me go," he said. *What a feeble negotiation.*

"Well now, that is the funniest thing I have heard all day," I replied, staring down at him. "A captain never abandons his crew, but you wouldn't know the first thing about that because you have never truly even been a captain."

I grabbed a knife from my pocket and dug its blades through the rope that tied his arms together. Harry already began to turn the wheels to loosen the ropes that held the boat up to our ship. As soon as Jean's hands were free of the rope, he attempted to climb out of it and back onto the ship.

"Oh, one last thing…" I said as I pulled Jean close to me and tugged off the red coat that had belonged to Captain Oliver. Harry got the other side and we stripped it off him so that he only had a dirty white tunic on and slacks. He had asked some of his crew men to put the coat back on him before we got rid of him. Since they had a closer relationship with him, they agreed to but still knew very well that he was a goner. Some crew could surely be loyal to the end no matter what.

"Wait, that's mine!" He called out and tried to climb out of the boat again. Harry went back to turning the wheel so that the boat lowered towards the seas. We continuously pushed him back until he was no longer able to attempt his escape.

"Wait!! Let's talk about this! I'll die if you leave me stranded in the sea! Come on, please!" He screamed in a pathetic attempt at forgiveness. We were passed that point. I still heard his screams as I walked back towards the stern of the ship to stare off at the paddle boat. Blessed William's towering sails sent us away from him until he disappeared from sight completely.

As I continued looking out at the open seas, land appeared in the light blue horizons. I brought out the compass that my grandfather had given me and saw that we were still heading Northeast to the coastline of America.

"What of Jack?" Harry came beside me to ask a question that was likely on everyone's minds.

"We will have a proper burial for him when we get to the land. Tell a few of our men to get some shovels ready so that we can mark his grave. He always wanted to come back to the Northeast," I said. It would have been best to bury him at Port Glasgow where he and I were both from, but there was no way that he would last that long to bring him back there. This would have to suffice, unfortunately.

"Aye, Captain," he said. I still had to get used to answering to that name. It still felt as though we were talking about Oliver when we referred to people as Captain as that is the only true captain I had ever known in my life. As we drew closer and closer to the land, I ordered a few of the mates to take down the sails so that we could slow down and throw the anchor into the depths of the water once we reached the docks. It seemed like all too quick of a ride, but just when I turned the wheel to reach the coastline of the Northeast, the island appeared close by and something in me took over, causing me to turn the wheel towards the forbidden land instead.

"Where are we headed?" Harry asked.

"Just over yonder. We can bury him here without any questions being asked and will be left at peace," I said. The answer came from me too quickly for I hadn't even known why I was headed that way either, but it is true that there would be many questions of why we were carrying a dead body onto land and how I was suddenly the captain of this vessel. The stories of the forbidden land irked me to my core, but this was our safest bet for the time being. It was daylight, which was much better than coming here at night as whatever I saw could've surely ripped us apart limb by limb. When we reached the shores, I alerted the crew to put out an anchor and we hopped into a few of the boats on the sides of Blessed William so that we could row the rest of the way to the island.

14

The perimeter surrounding the land was completely covered in sand and rocks. Bushes and trees marked the center, so you could not see all the way to the other side of the island. Looking from afar, it appeared much smaller than actually stepping foot on its sandy shores. White and grey seagulls soared high in the sky, mocking us in a way with their repetitive caws. It must have been humorous to them that we were unable to get to and from places as easily as they could. Remembering the stories and what I had seen from the mainland, I had reminded the crew to bring their weapons just in case.

"Why would we need those? There's no one here," one of them protested. It took them a moment to catch on, but then someone finally said it.

"Oh, it may be that ghost story that Captain Oliver used to tell…he's still scared," Harry said, grinning. I grinned back and then frowned right away showing that I was, in fact, serious. Even if the stories were fake, I did hear something that night when I was with Sarah. That much was undeniable. Sarah didn't even know that I was back in the Northeast. She would be surprised and likely saw that my ship was at anchor near the island. The questions in her mind must've been driving her crazy.

We headed towards the center of the island and I was glad that I brought my axe with me because I chopped various bushes down that were in our way, impeding our path. Stomping through the untouched soil felt liberating and reminded me of my days as a child in school when I used to daydream about this. Of course, my then child-mind over exaggerated some of the things that I hoped to find such as animals that I had never seen before, but what was even better was the fact that we didn't have to worry about anyone else on this land. There were no people to pass judgement, rules to follow or even a map to look at. The fact that we were blindly walking into this uncharted territory made my adrenaline rush all the same. I wondered what Jack would think about this because it would have been him that was by my side.

"Where are we taking him?" one of the crewmen asked. I looked down at my compass and saw that I had been heading Northeast as we started at the southern side of the island. All around us, there were nothing but tall grasses poking out of the grounds aside from the birds circling over our heads.

"Just a little bit longer. I want to see if there's an open place that we can bury him," I answered. Something within me said to keep going as there would be a clearing in the center of the land among the forest of trees. As the crackles of leaves beneath our feet sounded through the air, we kept moving forward until we found the open area in the center of the island. There were no trees here or even bushes or grass. Instead, an abundance of cleared dirt that looked as though it had been untouched lay before our eyes.

"How did you know this was here??" Harry asked as he handed a shovel to me. I didn't know what to say as I was just as spooked. Some of the other crew pitched in as we began digging a hole in the ground. The air around us felt cold even though it was in the middle of summer in the Northeast. As soon as we got to the center, the breeze that had been blowing through the air was gone and we couldn't even hear the waves any longer. An eerie silence other than shovels digging deep within the dirt sent chills down my spine. The rest of the crew didn't seem to be as affected, though, as they continued shoveling. When our hole was big enough, we all took one side of the large bag that contained Jack's body and tossed it down into the hole that was definitely big enough to fit all of us. One big grave for the entirety of the crew, unmarked... I shuddered at the thought and walked over to the nearest tree to look for something so that I could mark the grave with. Vines traveled up and around trees, appearing to choke and imprison them. Several other piles of dirt made me question if there were other burials in this space, however, there weren't any footprints. There was nothing to mark the grave with and I would have to go back to the perimeter of the island again to retrieve one. I looked in my bag and found the net that Jack liked to use when he fished and decided to use it instead. As the crew shoveled the soil back over Jack's concealed body, I dug the pole into the ground so that the net faced up right next to his grave. Although I had not been religious my entire life except for the times that I would be instructed to open the Bible at school, something overcame me and I began to whisper a prayer. It was the same prayer that I had said with my mother when father died.

"Saint Michael the Archangel," I paused as I heard the others join in although I had been whispering. We all continued the prayer, "defend us in battle. Be our protection against the wickedness and snares of the devil; May God rebuke him, we humbly pray; And do thou, O Prince of the Heavenly Host, by the power of God, thrust into hell Satan and all evil spirits who wander through the world for the ruin of souls. Amen."

When I looked around at the crew, I no longer saw strong, grown men. Instead, I saw lost children who now looked to me for direction. And it all made sense now. The prayer that I heard in school as a young boy finally fit life. No matter how you appear on the outside, everyone has a portion of themselves that is weak.

Whether it be from battle, hardship or loss, those that are fully exposed for their weaknesses and vulnerabilities could very well be slaughtered by the vultures of this world. The evil spirits that surround us are just preying upon that brief moment of weakness to take the reins in their hands and control us evermore.

I knelt beside the fishing net and traced my hands over where Jack would've normally held it as he showed me what I would be cooking for dinner that night for the crew. Although every day seemed the same to me, the amount of pride in his face never dulled as he seemed more surprised than I that he had caught something for us.

"Let's head back, cap't," one of the crew mates held out his hand. I looked up at him at first to protest as I had just wanted to stay there but seeing the concern in his face reminded me of the deep responsibility that I

held.

Too Late

15

Bumpy cobblestone streets full of shades of grey and brown from the dirt that surrounded seemed to match the gloomy day. In the distance, the island looked far more pleasing than where we stood as Jack's body was now there underneath the ground to stay for all of eternity. I had told the crew that we would stay for the day before setting sail again. It had been quite some time since I had seen Sarah and although I promised to write to her, it was difficult to stay in touch this way as I was always at sea. The last letter that I wrote was sent at one of our stops, but I wasn't sure if it ever made it to her. When I walked down the streets that still appeared the same as they had before, I remembered seeing a church right near the docks so I headed down in that direction. It was midday and the bells had rung, which usually came at the end of mass. Up ahead, there was a cross that stood erected from the top of a narrow building. I peered over my shoulder to see that Harry and a few others trailed behind me. A loyal crew. I had given them the day off and expected that they would go drinking, but instead they were here.

As we headed towards the church, I made the sign of the cross to show respect as I was taught in school by Mrs. Sarabella. Just as we were about to walk inside, a bride and groom came bustling out as everyone around cheered. We had been on the side of the groom who was all done up with a white wig atop his head which was common for wealthy men, especially when they were celebrating with others in the public eye. Harry suddenly stood in my line of sight and put his arm around me as to guide me in the opposite direction. I planted my feet in the ground and refused to walk any further.

"What are you doing? We'll be able to go in once they all walk out," I explained. They would go off to celebrate with food and drink so it was only a matter of time that they followed the bride and groom out.

"Let's go later, okay?" He said as he attempted to move me again. At this point, he must've known that I wasn't budging. "You're not going to want to see what's over there… don't say I didn't warn you." This made it even more evident that I turn around and find what was so off-limits for me to see. I broke his grasp on my arm and headed back towards the church. As the groom walked forward to open the door to the carriage, the bride stood there alone staring out at the crowds and waving. When she turned to her left, the same deep brown eyes struck me and in that moment, I wished I had listened to Harry's words of advice. There was nowhere left to turn as I felt shackled by her gaze. She looked as though she was surprised to see me and I had thought she would've seen my ship by the island long before, but all this time she had been preoccupied by something else entirely. Her long white dress trailed far behind her, all the way through the entrance of the church and her wavy hair was interwoven in a bun with a lacy white veil draped over the back of her head. Sarah's rosy cheeks now looked pale as if she had seen a ghost right before her. As the groom waited for her, he let out a cough to catch her attention as she broke her gaze and looked over at him. Sarah obeyed by walking onto the carriage and having a seat but looked back at me as he took his seat beside her. If it weren't for him being so occupied with talking to the coachman, likely giving directions as to where they would go, he would've surely caught sight of me. I walked over towards her side of the window to see the pout on her lips as she looked down. When the coachman whipped the horse, they began to take off and Sarah looked up, worry in her eyes as she went off with her new husband. She must've seen the hurt in my eyes as I could barely contain myself. If it weren't for my duty as a captain to my crew, I would've carried her off with me. We didn't have to ever go there again. We could have just left forever without a single glance back.

But there I stood as the coach raced away towards their destination, dragging up gusts of dirt to fill the air in an unbreathable smoke. I choked at my first attempt to breathe in and immediately turned around to walk down towards the docks. I didn't want to be there any longer and wished to set sail back towards England to get jobs done at sea which is what I did best.

"William, you'll find another girl," Harry attempted at comforting me. But that was the point... there was no other girl. This was the one.

"You guys go get some drinks, I'll meet up with you later," I attempted at putting a mask on by smiling but knew he could surely see right through it.

I headed for Blessed William so that I could just leave. It was clear that she had moved on and I wasn't wanted any longer. Waves crashing up against the sides of the vessel reminded me of when I first heard them as a young boy. The fight within me blared so loud back then. It had been so simple, though. I urged to do better than my father. A glimpse of deep purple led up by green stalks caught my eye before I headed onto the vessel. Bluebells. All of this, I had done for my mother back in Scotland. She still didn't know that I was captain of this vessel and if she heard, it would fill her ears with joy. I continued walking, but with a different plan in mind as I headed into the cabin. As soon as I sat in the seat, I took out the quill and began writing a letter.

Mother,

It has been long since I last sent a letter your way and spoke to you. So much has happened and I do not even know where to begin. Let me start by saying that I will end this letter very well and you will be proud to say the least. One unfortunate event occurred at sea and that is that Captain Oliver died. After that, a French man by the name of Jean Fantin took over as captain. Unfortunately, he was sent off the vessel due to his trying ways as a traitor. When the crew found this out, they made me captain. Mother, I am finally captain of the vessel. I have named it Blessed William because I am truly blessed and you have raised me well to get to where I am. I plan to come back to Port Glasgow in the months following and in that time, I will show you my vessel. I hope all is well.

With love,

"Captain" William Kidd

As soon as I put the quill down, a knock came from outside the cabin door.

"Come in," I stayed put and folded the letter, carefully sealing its the envelope. As I began to address it to Port Glasgow, Will came in. He was one of the crew mates and we would often just refer to him by the shorter name so that we didn't confuse his name with mine. When I became captain, it was much easier though. Will reminded me of my childhood friend,

Patch. He had many freckles all over his face and pink skin that easily burned in the sun. He only came on a few years after I had, but still had so much to learn. His red hair was long and went down to his shoulders. We'd usually keep him as a lookout for us while sailing. He'd be the first to warn us in any case of danger.

"Uh, cap't," he said, nervously as he stared down at his feet upon entering. He was one of the men we'd have to work with. There would be no way that he would survive a day out in the open on his own if he went acting like that... I made a mental note to myself as he fumbled to put his thoughts into words.

"Yes?" I asked. "Shouldn't you be out enjoying our day and night on land? Oh, don't find a girl on land whatever you do... rumor has it they move on pretty quickly."

"Harry and the guys wanted me to ask if you can come out with us. It'll be good for you," he finally blurted out. So, Harry put him up to this task. What did they think, I was in my cabin crying all alone? Pitiful… I felt myself growing angry the more I thought about her. Perhaps a night out would be what I needed — I'd wash away my memories of her with alcohol.

"Not a bad idea, Will," I said as I picked up the red coat that belonged to Captain Oliver previously. He walked over and helped me put each of my arms in a sleeve. Kissing up… I remember those days when I first boarded this vessel.

16

"Hey!!" Harry shouted out as he held a giant bottle that was already half empty. I quickly took a swig from it then grabbed my own at the bar. Will nervously sat on the other side of Harry but asked the bartender for his own cup of wine. As soon as I opened the cork to my bottle, I took a long gulp of the bitter liquid. It stung on the way down my throat, but the pain would be worth it at some point as I would forget my worries from before.

"How long have you all been here?" I asked. While Harry's plump stomach pressed into the table before him, Will looked like a twig. Harry's entire face was red and sweaty, revealing that he had likely been there the entire day drinking already. It was amazing how you could give your crew the day off, but they would choose to spend it in one spot drinking as they commonly would on the ship anyway. People were creatures of habit, always going back to the same routines or ways no matter how much they swore they wouldn't. I couldn't talk much about it as I would fall into the same trap. They all chuckled and drank even more.

"Oh, speaking of… this letter came for you," Harry said as he handed me a white envelope that was sealed by a gold emblem addressed from the English. It was interesting how they were able to find me in the

Northeast and at such perfect timing, too. Upon opening it, I realized it was from royalty. They requested my services and ship:

Captain William Kidd,

We have heard of your bravery with the previous captain and commend you and your loyalty to your crew. For this, we send an urgent request in this difficult time of Allegiance. As France seeks to widen its borders, we must protect what is rightfully ours. We propose you to begin privateering at once against any and all French vessels. It is with deep respect that we give you this job of protecting and liberty.

Sincerely,

Your English Ally

"When did you receive this?" I asked right away, trying to snap out of my already tipsy and woozy state. Harry shrugged his shoulders and got right back to drinking. He could really get on my nerves at times.

"Well, we leave at sunrise!" I brought the bottle of remaining alcohol with me as I headed out of the bar, expecting that they would be there the entire night leaving only to relieve themselves. Upon closing the creaking door behind me as they all started shouting a song that they would sing out at sea, I wandered off in the opposite direction of my ship. Deep down, I knew exactly where I was headed but wasn't sure why. Crickets buzzed in the shadows as the sun was setting in the horizons. As I continued down the path, I found myself on the all too familiar cobblestone that I should've never left from back when I still had the chance. Taking another swig of alcohol seemed like the best thing to do at the time as I threw the empty bottle down beside the path, quieting the crickets down. It likely hit some of them and the others were quite possibly getting drunk on the remnants that surely dripped out. I chuckled to myself thinking about it and heard the whinny of a horse from the barn. Wondering if Melody was still around, I ventured in, careful to look both ways as to not let anyone know that I was trespassing. Upon sliding the barn door open, I saw Melody's sleek coat and was delighted to see her. At least some things didn't change.

"Hey sweet girl," hiccupping after I introduced myself. As I wobbled over, I just hoped that she would remember. To my surprise, she put her head down and let me pet her just as she had so long ago. "Is it okay if I stay with you tonight?"

She snorted and pressed her head up to my chest. I continued stroking down her forehead towards her snout. This repetitive movement lulled me to the point that I felt the need to lay down and close my eyes even if it was just for a few minutes.

"I'll be right over there, girl" I said as if she could understand me. When I walked over, I noticed the blanket that I had used with Sarah that night that we'd fallen asleep together in the barn — something that would unfortunately never happen again. As I draped the blanket over myself and rested my head atop a pile of hay, it felt more like home than anywhere else. My eyelids felt heavier and heavier the more I strained to keep them open until I finally gave in and fell into a deep sleep.

Birds chirped endlessly, singing their unique songs to one another. The salty sea filled the air around me; I could almost taste its bitterness. It had a distinct scent that I grew all too fond of as it had been both my escape and savior. I lay on the ground in an open field of grass as the sun beamed down at me and for some reason, this was the only clearing as trees towered over my body. I looked down at the ground and my red captain's coat was nowhere to be found. Instead, I wore a loose, white shirt with a few of the buttons opened up and beige slacks. These clothes were similar to those that I wore before I became captain or even set sail. They closely resembled the hand-me-downs that I would wear as a boy back in Scotland. Rubbing my head, I felt as though I was in a different place. It was just a few moments ago that I lay in a barn with a horse nearby. But now, I was on what appeared to be an island with no sign of my crew.

"Hello?" I called out, feeling vulnerable and lost. I didn't have a musket with me nor did I carry anything else. A woman with deeply tanned skin peeked out from behind the tree and as soon as she caught sight of me, she hid behind it again. I began walking towards her, curious as to who she was and whether or not she was able to help me. She took off from where she hid, leaves crunching under her bare feet and I stopped in my tracks.

"It's ok, I'll stay put and let you come to me. I won't hurt you," I confirmed and did just as I said. She stopped running and glanced over at me, nervously.

Her tanned skin looked as though it had been kissed by the sun and she carried a wooden spear. The entirety of her face was adjourned in red and black face paints and the clothes she wore looked as though they came straight from a deer's fur and skin. She hesitated but stayed exactly where she was. Seeing her uneasiness, I decided to sit down on the ground to show that I meant no harm. She treaded towards me with the giant spear in hand and started to trace something in the dirt before me. I slowly stood up to see what she was drawing.

At first, it just looked like a circle then it had tall trees shooting out from the center of it. She traced a few lines above it and I thought those to be birds. Underneath the circle with the trees, she drew a line that looked as though it was a border. In between each of these, she drew curves that appeared to be waves. It looked like it was the forbidden island.

"The island?" I asked. She stopped tracing and looked right in my eyes then back down at the ground. At that point, she took her spear and stabbed it through the center on the ground aggressively and then drew a big "X" over the entirety of the island. As if I should've understood what that meant, she began to walk away with no explanation whatsoever. Suddenly, it felt as though a bucket of rain was being poured onto me as the sky opened up. What was a beautiful, sunny day turned dreadful and rainy. It came down so hard that my white shirt clung to my body.

I blinked a few times and heard a horse whinny uncontrollably in fear. The next time I opened my eyes, I found myself laying on the floor of the barn drenched in water. As I looked up, I noticed that part of the ceiling broke and the rain was coming down hard within the barn. I moved towards Melody and began to pet her, reassuringly.

"It's ok, girl. It's a bad storm and it will pass just like all the other storms of life do, too." My dream haunted me as I couldn't figure out what it meant. The girl marked an "X" over the island, which was forbidden. She was warning me not to come there again. That's what it meant. But why would I have a dream about that and who was the girl that I had never seen before?

"Hello??" the unforgettable, soft voice drifted into the barn as Sarah appeared in a white evening gown, rushing in from the storm.

Passion

<h1 style="text-align:center">17</h1>

She tripped over something on her way towards me and I caught her limp body in my arms. I had to remind myself that she was taken or I could've planted a kiss on her lips right then. Instead, I reluctantly helped her up on her own two feet again and she took the blanket from me, beginning to pat her dress. My eyes were glued to her as a magnet is to another. Her dark hair was as wet as mine and mirrored me in the way that it clung to her chest. Pale skin contrasted with the dark tones of her hair and eyes. A design made entirely of lace trailed from her shoulders down to her arms. I carefully set my hand on her side, using everything in me to hold myself back.

"What are you doing here?" she looked up at me in question.

"I could ask the same thing," I replied, playfully. She walked away and to the other side of the barn, lighting one of the lanterns in the corner as night was upon us.

"William… this is my barn. And shouldn't you be off on your ship?" she asked. This aggravated me as she knew that I would come back for her. I had promised her that I would.

"And shouldn't you be with your new husband?" I asked, curious…yet not so much as I didn't really want to hear about him. A man that had claimed the woman of my dreams? I did not need to know a thing about him. As soon as I mentioned him, she looked down at the ground and turned away from me, walking towards the window of the barn. This prompted me to follow her. As she peered out at the endless rain, I enveloped her in a hug, wrapping my arms around her from behind. She jumped where she stood then glanced over her shoulder at me. This made it even more difficult to hold back, so I walked away to keep the distance between us.

"This was an arranged marriage to one of the wealthiest men in New York...my parents set this up. He is about thirty years older than I and of bad health," she said. It didn't seem as though she wanted to be with the man and he did look much older than her, which was very common. Once that oath was made, there wasn't a thing that could break it, though. My hopes of marrying her had gone down the drain, unfortunately.

"I don't want to be with him, William," she turned around and laid her hand on my side. Whatever ounce of control that remained was now gone because I took her face in my hands and pressed my lips into hers. I could feel her hand slide up my wet shirt that still clung to my skin.

"Then be with me," I whispered and moved my lips down her neck, sending her head back in pleasure. She breathed in and out so deeply that I thought she would faint any moment. I backed away a few steps and pulled out something that I had in my pocket from mother years and years before when father had died. It was the ring that father had proposed to mother with and was passed down through our lineage. She had told me that

I should give it to the woman of my dreams. I remembered that when I asked her how I would know that all she could say was, 'When you know, you know...' I was already too late before, but I wouldn't be the next time — I was sure of that. When we first docked in the Northeast, it was the first thing that I placed in my pocket so that I would be able to use it as soon as I saw Sarah again, unknowing that she would already be married off.

As I took her delicate hand in my own, I slid the ring over her finger and it fit perfectly. Her left hand was bare as once you get married, moving the ring to your right hand was tradition. Now, she had rings on both hands. I knew that the one I had given her would be moved to the other side in only a matter of time.

"William, I can't…" she said as she began to take it off. I stopped her and intertwined my fingers with hers as I stood up again. I had to tell her how I felt this time because it was unpredictable whether or not I would be given another chance. Her sweet, concerned eyes were fixed on every move I made. I couldn't help but stare at her entire body as the gown she wore fit like a glove, accentuating every curve of her body.

"I don't want to be too late the next time. Keep this whether you have to hide it or give it to one of your friends to hold onto. I will come back for you and you will be mine," I said, pressing her down against the soft piles of hay. Feeling her body give into me as she became less reluctant to kiss me, I traced my fingertips up her side. She shivered and goosebumps formed along her arms.

"William, this isn't right," she pulled back. For one, it felt like it was meant to be, but she was right - she was a married woman now. She had made a promise to someone else. Everything that happened on the vessel and island thus far showed me how short life truly is. I wasn't sure when or if I would get another chance to show her how I felt and touch her the way that I was.

"Sarah, as long as the sun rises from the horizons — I will always feel this way about you. There is nothing more certain than that and I refuse to ignore it any longer. So, let me be damned — anything would be worth just one night with you," I pressed back into her as I felt her body release the tension it held previously. As we kissed, she pulled away and nibbled on my bottom lip playfully. I opened my eyes and locked on hers as she was full of desire. This urged me all the more to continue kissing her as my lips made their way down her neck and over her chest. She stood up and turned her back towards me, signaling me to unbutton her garments. Underneath, she had a tightened corset wrapped around her torso. I winced just looking at how tight it was. As I unraveled the laces of the corset, she let out a relieving sigh and wiggled out of her dress, stockings still on that went up to the middle of her calves. Although in her evening gown, she must've been in a rush to see what was going on in the barn outside.

"No one will find us here?" I asked as what I intended to do would not be quiet in any way, shape or form. She shook her head and came towards me, pulling my shirt up and over my head as she traced her fingers up and down my abs. The feeling of her hands on my body caused me to shudder and I just wanted even more. Her soft skin felt like clouds underneath mine. I pressed her down to the ground and began kissing the entirety of her body, taking my time with each kiss.

"William…" she said through gasped breaths, "I want you to be mine."

I brought my face back and pressed into hers, both of our bodies becoming one as she nearly screamed. As I held my hand over her mouth not to startle anyone, the horse remained quiet as if it didn't want to ruin anything for us. I felt the blood rush throughout my body and couldn't stop moving towards her and back again and again. Her head went back in pleasure, but I still held my hand over her mouth. It added a new level of excitement as I felt more and more in control. She pushed me towards the ground and we reversed positions. Now she pressed me into her as I lay there underneath her. Sarah's wet hair dripped down onto my chest and as she went faster, she took my hand and covered her own mouth. After just a few moments, her eyes bulged wide and she fell to my side, gasping for air.

"Oh no, dear..." she said, realizing what had been done.

The entire week had been a whirlwind as I woke up a crewmate with nothing to his name. Then, I became a captain and thought that I had lost the love of my life. If I could've chosen just one of those things, it would've surely been Sarah without a doubt even though I had always wanted to become Captain. There were no words that could express how I felt for her. As I rolled over, I kissed her on the forehead and her smile in response was all I needed.

"I need to tell you something… I am captain of the ship now," I said hoping I could tell her on better terms. She walked over to grab another blanket and laid it over both of us then snuggled closely by my side.

"Captain Kidd… that has a nice ring to it. I'm going to marry a captain…" she marveled at the sound of her own words. It made me smile at how proud she was of me. She traced circles over my bare chest and the flowery perfume was something I had been missing for far too long. It looked as though she was ready to fall asleep as her eyes closed and she breathed in and out slowly.

"Sarah…" I turned towards her and looked in her eyes as she had just opened them, sleepily.

"England has called me to seize French vessels. I must go at the crack of dawn tomorrow, but I promise you I will be back," I said, regretfully. A large part of me hoped that I would be back in time to be with her or that by some luck she would no longer be married to this man and we could just wed.

"I wish I could come with you," she admitted. Although part of me wished the same, it wasn't safe for her out there and a priority that was far more important than being a captain of a ship was keeping the love of my life safe.

"I will come back for you and we will wed, okay? You said that the man you have married is ill...so it is only a matter of time...but until then, we will just have to make do," I felt terrible for wishing for someone's death so that I could be with her, but it seemed to be

the only way.

War of Allegiance
18

Saying goodbye was the hardest part, but we had to go our separate ways in secret so that no one would see. At first, I felt that I had given up on all because the chance with her seemed to be gone. When she opened a door that I once thought was closed indefinitely, it made everything seem much more possible in life. Although I had barely gotten any sleep, I felt fully energized once I reached the ship at sunrise to depart with my crew. They had asked me why I was acting so chipper that morning and I felt as though they knew, but I decided not to reveal anything until it was a sure thing. We now set sail on The Adventure Galley which was given to us by the English. Along the sides of the ship were a total of thirty-four cannons. In addition to the men that already boarded the vessel, we now had around one-hundred-fifty crew mates. Three towering wooden masts soared high in the sky. The bowsprit held England's flag high in the air as its navy-blue background contrasted with red and white. As soon as we set sail, we headed towards England in search of French vessels. The calm seas always seemed to come just before some of the worst storms. We had privateered before, but never had the pressure of an entire country weighing down on our shoulders. During times like these, I took a moment to walk to the very edge of the bow, looking off as we sailed. Waves gently pushed the boat as we moved on; the wind guiding us through endless waters. The blinding sun peeked out of a multitude of clouds that masked the blue sky. Constant gusts sent the entirety of the sail back, billowing to its full extent.

"Cap't, I see a blue, white and red flag east of us," Will came rushing over.

"Steer 0, 9, 0," I replied, checking my compass.

"Aye Aye, Cap't," he responded and turned the wheel in that direction. As the ship followed, strong gusts of wind blew against the opaque sails. Their vessel was comparable in size, having three towering masts with sails out to their full extent and cannons along the sides. Although they could surely overpower The Adventure Galley with the abundance of weapons and crew, it was the act of surprise that would've likely won over tenfold.

"Raise the sails!" I urged my crew as they were quick to follow.

"Twice as many men as ours, cap't," Harry peered out from the stern of the ship with a long telescope, squinting his other eye. As we came around five or six ships' distance from the French vessel, I directed Will to steer so that the side of our vessel faced theirs.

"Get behind the cannons and get ready to fire!" At this point, they would've noticed that we were prepared to attack.

"Take cover!!!" I shouted as my men huddled underneath the outer railing, putting their hands over their heads as if that could protect them from the launch of cannons. In the next second, the French vessel shot a cannon right above the top deck, killing a couple of my men that were in its way, but it miraculously didn't touch the ship. It looked to be a warning from them since they hadn't struck directly through the vessel.

"Ready? Aim, FIRE!" I said as I grabbed a musket that I had retrieved while in America and began shooting the men on the opposing vessel one by one. At first, my aim wasn't steady in the slightest, but I had eventually gotten the hang of it as one of the men that I had aimed for fell over the side of their vessel. His body made a loud crash in the waters below. In the next moment, a few of my crewmates who were positioned behind the cannons of The Adventure Galley took the opportunity to fire them out. Their force caused the entirety of our vessel to vibrate as if it was shaking in fear from what had just come from our vessel. On the opposing side, one of the cannons had missed entirely while the other shot a deep hole within the heart of the ship, right through where the captain's cabin would be.

"Good work, lads, keep it going! Reload quicker!" I signaled some of the men that had muskets and rifles. As I walked past Harry, he handed the telescope over to me and I peered out at the French vessel, scanning for their captain. On the stern of their ship stood several Frenchmen with rifles of their own, carefully aimed and plucking my men one by one. I hadn't needed to, but when I returned the telescope, I aimed for the other men on their vessel before turning my musket towards their captain. I felt a deep rage overcome me that I had never felt before. I wanted to kill every one of them and leave no remnants whatsoever.

One of their cannons shot the very edge of the stern where I had just been a few moments prior. I shuddered at the sign that I had barely made it. They were clearly trying to target me since I was the captain. If they were able to shoot me down, they'd likely take over The Adventure Galley.

"Keep going!! Fire away!" The anger within me was fueled even more than a wildfire set to spread through the entirety of a forest. In the open sea, there was no way to contain it so there I was dropping men like they were nothing but mere flies in the wrong place at the wrong time. The remainder of the men on their vessel had ducked, careful not to be in the direct path of my ongoing bullets. They too fired back, but I kept moving positions so that they didn't have a clear direction to aim theirs. As I passed Harry again, I took the telescope from his hands and attempted at finding their captain another time but had no luck. They had stopped firing at us and at that point, I knew that it was time to completely relinquish anything that they had left. The center cannon on my ship laid empty with no one behind it. After carefully aiming it towards the center of the French vessel, I lit the very end and when the spark caught, its powder was quick to ignite as it launched in the exact spot that I had intended. White smoke flowed through the air after the initial fire as it sent its cannon towards their vessel. It tore through the main deck of their ship as men that had previously crouched to avoid bullets, now fell over the sides of the ship and in the middle where it began to break in half. At that, I whistled to what remained of my crew and called over to Will who had been closest to the wheel.

"Heave - Ho! North!" He followed and turned the wheel towards the French vessel. When we came about a ship's distance away, the crew momentarily put out an anchor as if they had read my mind. A few of us boarded the paddle boats that still remained on the sides and began heading towards the remnants of their battered ship. I paddled as fast as I could, unknowing of where I obtained the tremendous amount of energy after battling what seemed like it took hours. The disrupted waters splashed into the small paddle boats as we headed towards the French vessel. On the way, there were several men scattered about, hanging onto barrels and other broken pieces of their ship, clinging to life. A darkness had overcome me in that I did not give them a second glance upon passing by. Even during their screams for help, it only seemed to give me more strength and pride. Something had changed me after visiting the island and that shift caused me to lose much of my humanity in the way that I no longer cared. I was doing this for Sarah… to be with Sarah. So, my actions were justified and reasonable. As one of the French men closest to his own ship held onto a floating barrel, I took out my pistol and aimed right for his head, causing his body to go limp and eventually fall into the abyss of the ocean.

"What are you doing?" Harry asked from the other side of the paddle boat.

"Ridding the world of our enemy," I answered, grimly. This seemed to worry him as the troubled look on his face could've said a thousand words. He chose not to verbally say anymore as there clearly was no reasoning with me.

When we eventually came to their ship, I used a rope ladder to reach the main deck and Harry followed close behind with an empty bag to fill of various treasures. He had already begun to do so as I made my way towards what remained of the captain's cabin, looking for him. There was no sign.

"Cap't, look!" Will shouted from the stern of their ship. I walked over and peered out in the direction that he gazed to find one of the French vessel's paddle boats drifting away, further and further. The man in the boat had a trench-coat similar to the one that I wore and appeared to be a captain. He was making his escape. Without a moment's hesitation, I ran over towards the main deck and fired up their own cannon, aiming it towards the loan paddle boat that seemed to have thought it made it out. After a giant puff of white smoke filled the air, it drifted into their path and a colossal wave lifted up from the waters. When the smoke dissipated, there weren't any bodies to be found as just a few remnants of broken wood floated above the rocky water's surface.

Two-Sided Coin

19

A tremendous change had occurred when I was out at sea. The Adventure Galley had done its job and we collected treasures from England as promised. After that, privateering should have stopped, but for some reason my mind couldn't escape the deep darkness that surrounded me upon taking several lives. The blood on my hands made me feel that the damage had already been done and my soul was tainted forevermore. We set sail for the Northeast once again and I was prepared to wed Sarah. She already had her ring and it had only been a matter of time before she was widowed. Before docking along the coast, we took a similar detour as we did when we buried Jack.

"Lay the anchor," I called out to my crew.

"Aye, Cap't," they hollered back. The full moon shone high in the sky, illuminating the waters around us, causing an ethereal glow. What once had been dark, choppy waters turned into an open, vibrant world that awaited our explorations.

"Cap't, shouldn't we listen to the stories? This land is cursed," Will protested, nervously.

"We'll be quick," I reassured him, although it didn't appear as though he was calm. The others didn't protest as they thought that I was back to pay respects towards

Jack. That much was true, but there was also another purpose for our presence on the island. When we dropped the anchor, half the crew stayed on the ship and the remaining filed into the paddle boats to head towards the forbidden land. Two of the paddle boats mostly carried the treasures that we had earned from the English and some of which we had stolen from the French vessel. Harry and Will accompanied me in one of the other boats.

The sullen look on Will's face reminded me of the scared boy that I used to be, unable to stand up for myself. He paddled on, looking down at the shores that we headed towards. Will was the youngest of our crew at that point and didn't complain much, but also didn't reveal his story of why he was there. We didn't ask questions, though. Everyone had their reason for joining life out at sea, away from their homes and families. Most of us didn't even have homes to go back to, so it proved to be the only way. Just as before, I had instructed everyone to bring their weapons and this time, no one questioned why. It was as if we had all known that there was a mysterious creature that lurked on this island although none of us dared to say it aloud. An entire crew against one thing was not even a question of who would win or not. As long as I had my crew by my side, we should be okay.

"Let's gather the jewels," I called back to everyone as we reached the shallows. They seemed to know exactly what I had planned for they followed my direction right away.

I turned towards Harry and Will as they stood up, knee-deep in water and moved the boat further onto the beach.

"Let's keep our voices down just in case," I whispered. This alerted Will right away as he dropped the boat and it landed on part of Harry's foot. He hopped around, wincing in pain.

"I thought you said there was nothing to worry about," he said without whispering.

"Shh, yes. There isn't much to worry about, but we still need to keep it down. We're hiding some jewels in a place that we do not want anyone to find it," I quietly answered, annoyed at the fact that he chose not to whisper. If he was that scared of something being out there, he just gave us away. We might as well hold a flag and parade around in a line while singing. He shrugged and shook his head in disbelief at my response.

"We have half of a crew of men. We'll be fine," I muttered.

"But that's just a quarter of what we had prior. The French took so many of our men," Will pointed out.

"Still, several over one beast accounts for much more," I replied. Will shrugged then rolled his eyes.

Each of us hauled one of the bags as we headed towards the center. We took the same route that we had previously since I had already cut down the vines and bushes to create a walkable pathway. As we edged the forest of trees within, there was no path to be found. Instead, the bushes and vines were just as they were, as if we hadn't been there at all. I handed my bag over to

Harry and took out a blade to begin cutting a way for us again.

"Didn't we already do this?" Harry asked the obvious. I shrugged and continued cutting as my crew followed closely behind. It seemed as though it was taking forever to cut the vines and I felt dizzy with confusion as we had just done this not too long ago when we came to bury Jack's body.

"Hey, does anyone know where Will has gone to?" One of the men asked. I stopped cutting vines and bushes to look back and counted everyone. There was no scream or any rustling about, so he was likely fine.

"He was scared. Probably went back to the boats," I shook my head, barely able to believe my own words of reassurance.

"Let's just bury it here," Harry suggested.

"We must move forward," something pulled me towards the center no matter how scared I had been. It was almost as strong as my need to be at sea. As I chopped the bushes in our way, we eventually came to a similar clearing as we had the last time. Not one bush in the center. Nor a single tree. It defied every law of nature and did not make an ounce of sense. One of the men moved before me as I just stared into the still air at nothing… nothing at all.

"Where is Jack's grave?" One of the men asked the exact thought that ran through my mind. In the next moment, the calm that had once surrounded us diminished as screams pierced the air.

"HELP! CAPTAIN! CAPTAIN!" The familiar young voice called out from the way that we had come. I hadn't heard a voice in such distress since Jean Fantin begged for his life. However, this man was different because he was one of my own. Will was similar to a son that I had always wanted to have, but never did. The mystery of what happened to Jack's grave was soon pushed to the back of our minds as we now had a new problem on our hands.

Without warning, I fled the clearing from the center and headed back down the path that brought us there in the first place. This time, I didn't worry about keeping quiet as I ran towards the screams. Shuffling to load up the musket so that it was ready for whatever caused Will to scream, I had eventually reached the outskirts of the island and found myself alone in silence. Waves washed shells in and receded back, nothing affecting them in the slightest. The wind's cool whisper traced down my spine, causing my entire body to tremble. As

I looked out at the open seas, confused, I longed to be back on The Adventure Galley so that I could feel at home again. What I would've done to go back and live life as it was before we took the French vessel and lost many of our men... The moon shone out over the waters and served as the only light that guided me back to that home. While I had thought my crew followed close behind me when I went to follow after the screams, no one was there.

"Will?" I called out, hoping for an answer. Deep down, I knew better than that though. After the screams that blared out, he had surely been in life threatening danger. Although it had been tempting to take a paddle boat and just go back towards The Adventure Galley, I turned in the opposite direction and decided to walk around the outside of the island until I found an answer.

As I crept closer and closer, the sand pressed down beneath my feet and I felt as though I was sinking and at some point, I would become buried on this land along with Jack... wherever he was. A gut-wrenching scrape sounded from nearby as I hesitated to turn back but knew that I had gone too far to do so. Trees swayed in the wind as a sudden movement came from behind. Lifting the musket, I stood ready for whatever was to come although I had the disadvantage of being out in the open. In the next moment, the rounded body of one of my crewmates came out, frantically. I had been so close to firing the musket but pulled back at just the right time as not to accidentally shoot him.

"Captain!" He ran my way and grabbed both of my wrists, shaking me as if he were trying to wake me up from a long nap. My eyebrows lifted in confusion.

"The men are… the men are…oh captain, help us," he continued and got onto his knees as he said the Hail Mary over and over again. I picked him up from where he knelt, wanting answers.

"The men are what?" I asked. What had normally been a jolly drunk turned into a man who was now scared of his own shadow.

"Dead. They are all dead," he looked down and sobbed uncontrollably slobbering into his handkerchief. Being captain of the ship, even on land I refused to abandon my own. As I left to go back towards the center of the island, Harry's sobs faded until I could no longer hear him at all.

Piracy

20

The energy had drained from me completely. The only thing that I ran on was pure determination and nothing else because of the lack of sleep and coherency as to what was happening to my crew. My mind went to Sarah and her smooth skin. The moonlight's reflection in her eyes that night, causing them to twinkle, was a sight that I could've died looking at and have been happy that I just saw them once in my entire life. But I had made a promise that I would be back for her and fully intended on keeping it.

As I drew closer and closer towards the clearing, I no longer took the path that I had cut down and my clothes ripped from the various thorn bushes that stuck out. I hadn't the time to cut a new path as my crew needed me.

When there were no more bushes and thorns poking out of the grounds, I realized that I finally reached the clearing. It was no longer a grave for Jack alone… Before me was a sight that I never would have imagined in my worst nightmares. Several torn bodies lay mangled about. An unrecognizable swarm of limbs had been thrown this way and that. When I saw Will's arm as I walked through the battle zone, I couldn't help but vomit all that remained in my stomach. An eerie silence wrapped itself around the cool air and left me even more alone. The clouds had passed over the moon, causing no light whatsoever. As I continued walking, it was difficult to make out some of the bodies and who they had belonged to. The clouds had drifted passed and the full moon set out a spotlight over me. I felt as though I would be next to be taken by whatever beast lurked on this island. Passing by several mangled bodies, I was now able to recognize some of my crew by the garments they wore. Most of their torsos had fresh blood seeping out of tears on their shirts. What once had been white tunics were now darkened and tarnished. None of the treasures were anywhere to be found that we brought onto the land in hope of burying for safe keeping. None of that even mattered now; what good was a captain without his crew? A storm could've rolled through and done less damage to them than whatever creature did this. *Why was I the exception along with Harry?*

"Take Me!" I shouted at the night sky. My words echoed through the clearing, but no response came. When I could barely stand it any longer and found that there was nothing more I could do, I regretfully began to turn back. Just before I came to the forest of trees that surrounded the clearing, I passed by Will a second time. Unable to look for very long, I briefly noticed one of his arms as it lay over the musket that I had given him long ago and taught him how to use. I felt a tear stream down my cheek as it should have been me that was mangled to death and not this young man who still had his entire life ahead of him. I walked over and carefully took the musket from underneath his arm as it dropped to the ground, limp. Wishing that I could somehow turn back time and make things right, I continued to head back towards the vessel. The prickers that had previously torn through my clothes didn't have much of an effect on me now as I just felt numb and hollow. The last time that I felt this way was when I lost my father and my entire life was shaken up as if the devil took the world in his hands and decided to throw it around. As I stepped over various twigs and bushes, the crunch of broken leaves was the only sound that filled the air. When the crashing waves sounded in the air, I followed it as a firefly would to light. At one point, I stopped to check my compass so that I could ensure I was heading towards The Adventure Galley and the crunching of leaves ceased. A strong breeze passed by me and the whistling wind sent a chill down my spine as it had earlier. Although I stood still, the crunching of leaves sounded again from behind me. I glanced back and saw nothing, but stayed exactly where I was, frozen with fear. The steps continued and when I was able to hear them more, I knew that they were coming even closer to where I stood. This time, I turned around completely and held up the musket that I had just taken from Will's dead body and aimed in every direction that I could, unable to tell where they were coming from as the sound surrounded me now. Beyond the trees, there was a distinct glow that illuminated in a single spot. As it drew closer, I saw what it truly was in its entirety. From behind each tree, mangled bodies that looked as though they were sewn back together somehow crept towards me. Bony fingers extended from their torn clothes and within the tears were bare skeletons protruding out, no flesh concealing what lie beneath any longer. Soulless bodies treaded towards me and their lack of humanity masked whoever they once were. It felt like my feet dug into the ground as I was unable to move. The sudden shock paralyzed my body with fear. One of the skeletons seemed to be leading everyone else and that's when I noticed the satchel that lay over its shoulder. Will's satchel. He came an arm's length away from me and ripped the musket right out of my hands. If it was Will, he wouldn't have turned on me but somehow he was able to speak grumbled words.

"Stay with us, you stay forever," he said as he pointed the musket back at me. In that, I snatched it out of his arms and began to run as fast as I could through the trees and towards the shore. I didn't look back once. When I reached the outside of the island and heard the calm of the waves, Harry was paddling off to go back on the vessel..

"Wait! Wait!" He looked back, but continued paddling. I treaded water until I was about neck-deep and caught up with his paddle boat, lifting myself into it.

"Why didn't you wait?" I screamed, gasping for air like a fish out of water. He was still paddling as fast as he could, towards The Adventure Galley.

"And let them take me too? No, thank you!" He announced. He had a point. I looked back towards the island and could see the glow of the skeletons that remained of some of my crew, but they stood on the outskirts of the island. A cloud covered the moonlight and I could no longer see them as if they were never even there.

"So you saw them too?" I asked, attempting to ensure that I wasn't crazy.

"What do you think I was running from?" He snapped. "I want to go back on the ship and never take another look at that island ever again.

"In fact, I may just stay away from the sea when we get onto the mainland," he continued as he grunted and handed me the paddles to continue going. It was not very likely for a crewmate to stop his life at sea. But this had my complete understanding, although I could never leave my life as a captain.

"Harry, I don't know what is going on with our crew, but let's just try to dock on the mainland and get to safety," I said.

Mainland

21

The crew didn't seem to believe Harry nor I when we explained what happened with the others that had accompanied us onto the island. A few of them burst out laughing and some of the others commented on the fact that we both had to stay away from the rum for a while until we got back to our senses. We just looked at one another and walked off, both knowing very well what we had just seen. The tides picked up quite a bit as we headed towards the docks and I wanted to find Sarah as soon as possible whether she was with the man that she had married still or not. Just like it had been any other night at port, Harry and the others went off to drink together in the bars while I walked to the home that Sarah's family used to own, right where the barn had been. The cobblestone path that was all too familiar was still there and I could hear the horse stomp its feet from within the barn as I passed. This time, I wasn't going to the barn and instead right to the main house that I had never stepped foot in before. Although it had been late, I knocked on the door as loud as I could, not caring if it disrupted the man that she had married or not. I needed to see Sarah right away.

After a few more incessant knocks, I saw the glow of a candle from behind some curtains as it drifted through one room. With a hesitant creak, the door slowly opened and Sarah was behind it, holding a small child in her arms and the candle in the other as she set it in a holder that was on the wall beside the door. I felt as though my heart was going to give out any second. This was the cherry on top of surprises for the night.

"Hello?" I asked as if she was a new person that I had never met before. Sarah still had the same long, wavy brown hair and deep brown eyes to match. Her nightgown came down low to her feet and she wore a white robe over it. The child that she held in her arms looked as though she was at least two years of age. She turned back towards Sarah, pressing her face into the skin of her neck out of fear as she didn't know who I was. From what I could see, her brunette hair resembled Sarah's, but because she was faced the other way I couldn't see much more than that.

"Mommy, I scared," the child said, clearly distressed from being woken up in the middle of the night, too.

"William," Sarah said my name and her sweet voice was music to my ears that I had missed for far too long.

"Let me set Cataline down to bed again and we'll talk," she said. I had wanted to vent to her about everything that I had just seen with my crew and the French vessel that we sunk and stole jewels from, but it seemed like she had even more to tell me. She turned around and picked up another candle, lighting it from the one that she had placed on the wall. As I followed her in, there were several seats in the main area of the house so I slumped down in one of them, finally giving into the exhaustion from the day's events, but here I felt safe. I was surprised that Sarah let me in being that she was a married woman still. The room was mostly bare, except for some wooden tables and an iron stove for cooking. On the opposite side of the room was a tall fireplace that was adjourned with the similar cobblestone to the path that I had used in order to come here.

"William," she said again coming over towards me as she sat in the chair next to mine. She wrapped her robe closer to her body as if she was cold.

"I told you I would come back," I said, explaining my presence. Despite having a nightgown on, she was still the most elegant person I had ever laid my eyes on. Somehow, she made her robe even look fancy. The sleeves hung down over her arms and hands, concealing them. She reached her arm up to her cheek wipe a tear from her eye and that's when I noticed my mother's ring on her finger that I had given her.

"Where's your husband?" I asked, wondering how he could have possibly been okay with this.

"He's right here," she smiled at me as she showed the other hand from her sleeve that revealed no ring at all. So, the only ring that she wore was the one that I had given her.

"The man that I had married died shortly after you left. I told you he had been ill and just didn't want to die alone which is why he married me and it was arranged. I was his company for a short duration," she finally gave more of an explanation this time. The years at sea had gone by so quickly for me, but here it seemed that so much had happened in my time away. She was completely alone and without a husband, but here she was telling everyone that I was her husband. I walked over to where she sat and took both of her hands in mine as she stood up to face me.

"Sarah, you have waited all this time for me?" I asked and before she could answer, the sound of the wind whistling caused me to jump. It reminded me of what had come shortly after on the island.

"What's wrong?" She asked, concern filled her eyes as she usually saw me in a more protective way as opposed to scared. I felt that I had to show strength so that she knew she was safe, but here I was just as anxious as the little child who lay in the other room.

"There are things on that island that you wouldn't ever imagine in your wildest dreams. Things that I can barely explain. I lost some men out there and it has been a very difficult voyage these past years," I said, unable to figure out a way to tell her what had truly happened.

"Sarah, I'll be wanted over here... there's just no other way," I continued and started sobbing. She held my head to her chest and rubbed my back in a circular motion.

"William, come to bed with me... you look like you haven't had a night's rest in a while. I'll be by your side the entire night," she said. I was grateful that she didn't ask me to explain further because it was difficult to say the meager number of words that I had. She blew out the candle on the wall and used the other as she took my hand. As she guided me down the opposite corridor from where she had gone with the child, we passed several rooms. At the very end, she brought me to a room with a bed that had been half-made as my incessant knocks had woken her up. The white sheets were far better than the hay that we were used to meeting at each time in private. A pan underneath warmed the entirety of the bed and I felt my body loosen as I laid back. Sarah blew out the light and the only glow that remained was that from the moon that shown in from the nearby window. She had gone over to the other side and laid while staring at me as if I was a star that had just come down from the heavens. She had been waiting for me all this time not knowing whether or not I would even make it back in one piece. It must have been rather difficult. Trying to go to sleep in this bed alone each and every night was likely torture. And to care for a child… I couldn't help but feel a deep jealousy that she bore a child with another man.

It just didn't feel right, but what was done was done and there was no turning back.

"William," she whispered and I turned towards her. As we had both been welcoming one another and talking about the time that we had missed in each other's lives, we hadn't gotten a chance to touch as much as I wanted. A loose strand of hair fell over her face like it had been a piece of soft silk. I gently took it in my fingers and put it behind her ear so that I could see her face.

"Come here," I pulled her closer to me and pressed my lips into hers. Her smooth legs enveloped around me as I guided my fingers along her nightgown. Her soft, white gown allowed me to feel every curve of her body. When I traced my fingers back up, I felt her breasts in my hands and began to make my way down but this time, with my lips. I could feel her body shiver. She pulled off my shirt and threw it to the floor and I moved off the bed to stand so that I could strip myself down. There was no stopping me at this point. The fear that struck me to my core was now pushed to the back of my head as she clouded my mind like a potent drink. Unable to control myself, I pressed her down onto the bed and as she gasped, I gave her part of the blanket to stifle her moans. Her head pressed back into the sheets as I pleasured her and myself at the same time. At one point, she had finally opened her eyes and I stared deep into her. The blanket was beside us and she reached her arms up and wrapped them around my back, pulling me down towards her. The closer that I got, the more she dug in her fingernails. It wasn't a bad pain in that I knew it meant I was pleasuring her. When her chest pressed against mine and we were the closest we could be to one another, her body jolted at the same time mine did and a rushing wave came over our bodies. I rolled over and laid beside her as we both breathed heavily. When I turned, I intertwined my fingers in hers and she laid her head against my bare chest. We both drifted into a deep darkness.

Inherited
22

The nature of being is to pass on something to the world. Whether it be knowledge, memories or a family, every single person has something that they give and leave after they are gone. In that sense, they are never truly gone as what they have passed on is carried through generations whether it is directly noticed or not. When one finds their version of home, that is when they have a true sense of belonging. For a home is a safe place that you can be who you are without feeling the need to put a mask on. It is a place that you are no longer judged and instead, accepted for the entirety of your being. Although the seas had turned into a home for me, I had come to realize that a home was no longer a building or vessel. Instead, home was who you were with when you felt that way — when you could be yourself. That is when you are the freest. In essence, it could very well be many different places. Right now, my home was by Sarah or anywhere that she was. When I was with her, I was somehow back in my father's house in Greenock, Scotland. But I was also on my vessel. The one thing that those had in common was that they were all places that made up who I was and where I felt the freest.

As I lay in the bed, I turned towards Sarah and just watched her, not wanting this moment to ever end. The sun had slightly peeked over the horizons which was my favorite time of the day because of the memories that I had grown fond of when I was a young boy, peering out at the ships. Sarah blinked a few times and stretched her arms out, hugging me.

"Hello," she smiled, yawning the second half of the word.

"Hi there, pretty lady," I smiled at her. Even when her hair was all tangled from rolling around in bed, she was still the most beautiful sight that I had ever seen. Several strands of messy hair now hung over her face. We both had blankets over our bodies. A knock came from the other side of the door. It was gentle and we would've missed it if not for the silence in our conversation.

"Mama," the child slowly opened the door and poked her head in, shyly. She looked like a miniature version of Sarah if not for the eyes. The piercing green eyes. I looked over at Sarah and then back at the girl. I had seen her previous husband and he had brown eyes that had been darker than Sarah's. They appeared to be almost black.

"Go sit at the table and I will be right out for you, okay?" Sarah said. The child obeyed and closed the door behind her.

"When were you going to tell me?" I asked, knowing very well what I saw. She squeezed her eyes shut as if she had hoped to hide it from me.

"Right away, but I couldn't last night," she said as she stood up and went into the wooden wardrobe along the wall to search for day clothes.

"Why not?" I asked, curious and still upset that I hadn't known.

"William last night was hard for both of us and it wasn't the time," she explained as she took off her nightgown and placed a day dress over her head.

"So I am right?" I asked, still pressing my theory.

"William, she is yours. But we can't tell her that because people will notice that I had an affair with you while I had just married him," she admitted. I stared up at the ceiling not knowing what to say or do because nothing could give back the time that I had missed and I would have to set sail once again and be away from them at some point.

"She can't know?" I wondered what I could've said to change her mind. Surely we would have more children and they would bear my name. Sarah just shook her head. I finally regained my senses and put on my clothes that I had worn the previous day.

"You can raise her like you are her father, but she can never know you are her true father..." she said. Clearly she had thought this through herself and it didn't seem like she was budging on her decision. It may have been for the best because a child born out of wedlock was not respected in the slightest and at least if she bore her previous husband's name then she would have somewhat of a decent reputation. In fact, it would be much better off given that I was likely known as a pirate for the vessels that I had taken and sunk.

"Let's go out, you can say hi," she said. My heart raced so fast and although she was barely three feet tall and a child, I was frightened. I nodded and we headed out towards the kitchen.

"Cataline, this is William," she said and I came out from behind her to wave as if I had lost any words to speak. She waved back at me and continued playing with a small doll that looked as if it was sewn together. There was a toy wooden boat that she also had next to the doll. When I saw this I looked over at Sarah and she seemed to read my mind.

"I had to get her a boat; it only made sense," she admitted. I was proud of this because it meant that Sarah planned for me to be in her life all along. She must have known the entire time, too. I walked over to her and looked closer at her toys. The boat had "The Adventure Galley" carved into its side.

"What do you have there?" I asked. She placed the doll in the boat and started moving it around.

"My ship," she explained. She thought she was a captain. If she hadn't the same green eyes that I and my mother had, I would've still thought she was my own.

I felt a tear stream down my cheek and in this moment, I felt exactly what my mother and father had felt when they had me. There were no words as I just watched her in utter admiration. She placed her doll in the toy ship and rocked it back and forth as if it was in choppy waters during a storm.

"William, can you run into town to grab some fruit?" She asked almost as though I had been there every single day and it was just an average stroll out that I would commonly do. The normality was something that I could use.

"Sure," I stood up from where I had just knelt and began to walk towards the door.

"Will you be back?" The little voice asked.

"Always," I answered.

Cursed
23

Legend says that when Captain Kidd went out that morning, he did eventually return. But he was never the same. The island seemed to call to him each and every night. Sarah would find him sleepwalking in that direction. One time, he had gone so far as half of his body was covered in water as he tried walking towards the island. Although he lost half of his crew there, the remaining half stayed on The Adventure Galley with him as they set sail several more times to capture vessels and privateer. Word traveled fast and he was soon wanted for the capturing of several vessels in the Indian Ocean. People say that William went back to the forbidden island time and time again. When he went to the center, something in him was lost to the island and never reappeared. It was as though his soul stayed tangled within the forest of trees on the forbidden land. At one point, Sarah had written letters to Port Glasgow to warn him not to come back or he would surely be captured. He hadn't listened and always came, returning his promise. As Sarah grew sick, he became more and more worried of her mortality and it seemed as though he attempted at bargaining with the spirits of his old crew that remained on the island. Like a deal with the devil, he had attempted at negotiating everlasting life. Upon his return, whatever was left in him that remained human had diminished as he grew cold and distant. The governor of Massachusetts found and captured him while he didn't shed as much as one tear upon his arrest. The people that were caged beside his jail cell said that he would often talk to a man by the name of Will even though he was completely alone in his cell. They would ask him why he was talking to the air, but he would simply ignore them and continue speaking gibberish. After he was unable to stand for himself in the courts, he was hanged. Mother hanged too for being an accomplice as I had opened up her very last letter to me on my eighteenth birthday, having to raise their other two children on my own.

Cataline,

It has been a long time that I have carried this burden and if you are reading this, it means that I am gone and was not able to tell you in person. When you were conceived,

I had just married a man that was of ill health. Out of

passion and a failed attempt to escape from love's hold, I

spent a night with William Kidd. The next day, he

returned to sea and I didn't see him for several years. A

month or so after this, I found that I was bearing a child.

I wanted to tell him, but he was always out at sea and the

only address that I had for him was his hometown in

Scotland which he did not travel to as frequently. Cataline,

I am telling you this because you are the daughter of

William Kidd. Now, you must keep this secret. You must

not tell a soul. His name has been slaughtered due to

pirating. Cataline, just know - that your father loved you

with every ounce of his being.

Yours truly,

Sarah Kidd

Upon reading that letter, everything had clicked and made sense. When the other children came of age, I left the house that mother passed onto us and searched for any remnants of my father's life. Many days, I had walked outside and peered out at that island that had driven him mad. Full of wonder, part of me longed to go out there to see if he truly was mad or if he had been telling the truth the entire time of the souls that were trapped there. One morning when the sun was just appearing from the horizons, I noticed a vessel as it was just leaving from the forbidden land. I ran towards the sandy shores of the mainland as fast as I could to see who it was and pulled out a telescope that father had left with me due to my growing interest in sailing. As I peered through the telescope, I was able to get a closer look at the inscription on the side of the vessel:

The Adventure Galley

Acknowledgements

Thank you to those that I have lost for always sending reminders even when you are no longer here physically. I couldn't have done this without you.

I am grateful for the Maryland Writing Association for providing countless workshops and networking opportunities to learn more about publishing and writing.

Thank you to my family and friends for supporting me on my writing journey and always cheering me on. I couldn't do it without you!

Charles Island Disclosure

Charles Island is located in Milford, Connecticut and is a state park. The sandbar (tombolo) between Silver Sands State Park and Charles Island over washes twice daily with tidal flooding which produces dangerous currents and undertow. No one should walk on any portion of the tombolo when it is covered with water.

Attention Hikers!

It is important to know walking all the way to Charles Island is not always possible. Low tides do not always uncover the tombolo completely. See Milford Harbor/Connecticut tide chart for tide details.

<u>NO CROSSING May 1st to September 9th due to natural area preserve for nesting birds!</u>

Remnants

1

Moisture filled the air with an unnerving taste of confusion and desperation for what once was. Every lone droplet of rain gathered on earth's impenetrable surface, softening its grounds. The consistency of each drop altered shortly after they absorbed into one another. This ongoing charade reminded me much of humanity as we would all eventually become something bigger than just ourselves…or that was the hope, anyway. A horrifying image of the ruined remains of what used to be my life laid before me. As the rain showered down on me, I squeezed my eyes and clenched my jaws — hoping that when I reopened them, I could awaken from the nightmare that my life had become. It is said that rainwater has a purifying property and will cleanse all. The woes and broken promises of yesterday were forgotten, or at least pushed to the back of my mind as I struggled to grasp reality. I felt my hair becoming more and more soaked as I stood there, unable to move — barely able to stand completely on my own. My long, brunette strands clashed against the white of my dress. It had taken me hours and hours to prepare for the perfect day that would come to its crashing demise.

As a young girl, I would hear the church bells sing in celebration of two people coming together. Whenever those chimes would sound, I'd rush to the window on impulse and look out, waiting for the horse and carriage to stampede down the roadway. From the house that I grew up in, we were just close enough to see the outside of the church. A woman would appear from its colossal doors beside the man that had courted her. Her white dress puffed out under her torso with layer upon layer concealed by a sheet of white lace. Its sleeves fit like a glove, reaching down to her wrists in a frilly design that I made a mental note I would never have if the day were to ever come for me. White lacing to match the entirety of the pure dress tied in a bow on her back, it looked almost painful to wear. Her veil swooped back and trailed behind her, laying delicately over the back of her dress and blending with the lace. At the start of her veil were various flowers. Her neck was adorned in pearls that clashed eloquently with the darkness of her hair, which had been pulled back in several braids intertwined into one another. But more important than any fancy dress was the fact that it was a day that she and her man would come together as one. Oftentimes, I would see couples that didn't seem to have much interest in each other. One time, there was a man that stood beside his bride and I would see him staring off at other women that very day! But…on rare occasion, you would see a man and a woman that couldn't tear their eyes off one another. There would be a twinkle in his eyes, as any onlooker could tell he thought the absolute world of the woman he was with. That right there was the kind of love I wanted to find…

I shook my head as to snap out of the flashback for this day should have been the one I had been waiting for my entire life, possibly being an inspiration for another girl like I had been all those years ago. It had the most perfect start, but all storms come after a brief calm.

After the emergency bells sounded, the first thought that came to my mind was to find the man I was destined to marry and make sure that he was okay. The rush of the waves matched my initial attempts at finding him. Corridors lay before me, destroyed and in an irreversible state of ruin. The doors and any remaining exits were inaccessible as fallen pieces of roof had blocked any and all openings. When I woke up that morning, I would have never been able to guess that the day would have turned out this way. I knew all too well what would happen after they repeatedly warned me. When the others weren't spelling it out, there were other signs as clear as day. The stubborn nature of my being ran deep within me and there was no way to refuse its temptations. At first, the warnings came to me in dreams and I was quick to shrug them off as just pointless worries. As commoners reported the strange occurrences throughout their visits, there was always some type of excuse to explain their confusions. But no, now it was too late to go back and listen to that very first sign that could have helped to avoid all the damage that lay before me and scorched my mind by replaying the devastating memories again and again.

At first glance, the land before us stood full of promise and anticipation. No more worries of the past and a new life to build from the ground up. It had been years since my father and I were on our own, but we made do. When our ancestors came to America, they had been promised the streets would be paved in gold...it forced my mind to wander and form unrealistic expectations of the new place that we would soon call home. When you have lived in a certain place your entire life and unexpectedly make the journey elsewhere to start anew, it is both frightening and exhilarating at the same time. The horrors of the unknown lurk in the depths of your mind, but they are quickly suppressed by pure imagination of the incredible what-ifs to come.

Forget all of that, though. None of that matters now…or at least anymore. I struggled to keep my back straight as I looked before me. The heat radiated from within the center of the land. Violent patterns of red and orange billowed in the wind as it spread like a contagious disease, extending throughout the entirety of the island. Relentless waves of smoke stormed out from what once were windows that people would sit by to enjoy the outside air. Flames danced in the wind as it blew them left and right, causing them to spread like a sudden, dismantling toxin. As it flickered in each direction, it seemed to mock us — dancing in the constant gusts. A deep pit in my gut felt as if it would consume the entirety of my being. I longed to run as fast as I could from what I once thought to be my home. The surrounding waves echoed, reminding me of my own inability to escape the land's demise. But what poisoned me even more than my imprisonment was my longing to go back to when it all began. The simple journey that had just begun all those years ago. An ordinary life didn't seem so bad after all compared to the fate that now wrapped around me like permanent chains, weighing me down.

Trees that had once towered over me like tall buildings were torn apart by flames, which sent them tumbling down. Seagulls that soared high in the sky yesterday, abandoned their homes and were nowhere to be found. The absence of life caused the land to become eerie and uninviting. Powerful waves clashed against the outskirts of the coast, adding to the repetitive rumble of trees as they demolished a building in the center with their weight. They pressed it down firmly until it no longer looked as though it was a building, but instead a war zone. Water began trickling down from the sky as if those above cried out for the unfortunate souls below. Even this could not delay its demise; for a curse seemed to linger on this land.

Invisible shackles held me there, forbidding my escape both in mind and body. There was nothing to do except hold on to the meager amount of humanity that still remained within.

Stay tuned for more in the Tales of Charles Island series!

About the Author

Marissa is the author of a memoir and the Tales of Charles Island series. Marissa mostly writes fictional stories and began by journaling and writing screenplays in elementary school for her peers to perform. She spends much of her time with her pets aside from traveling to new places and journaling. Born and raised in Connecticut, she holds New England close to her heart and many of her stories are based in the suburbs of Connecticut. She has a deep and profound respect for people with special needs as her first job in her field was a special educator. Marissa found her voice through writing. While in high school, she was the editor of the Arts and Entertainment section of the school newspaper. She pursued a degree in Education, minoring in English literature and Anthropology. Later, she went back to school to better understand Autism and graduated with a Master's in Special Education.

Marissa would love to hear from you. Use the links below to connect & hear about upcoming books:

Visit Marissa's Website:
https://www.mystywrites.com/

Instagram:
https://www.instagram.com/_mysty_writes/

MARISSA D'ANGELO